THE OUTLAW OF LONGBOW

Rush Wisdom was condemned to the hell of the Territorial Prison at Yuma for the murder of his own brother. He broke his shackles and crashed out, over a precipice and down into a wild, flooding river. He was determined to find the man who had killed his brother, and as they were saying in Longbow, "If Wisdom got out alive, he'll be after you. Tomorrow. Or the next day, or the next . . ."

THE OUTLAW OF LONGBOW

Peter Dawson

GUNSMOKE

First published by Collins

This hardback edition 2004
by BBC Audiobooks Ltd
by arrangement with
Golden West Literary Agency

ISBN 0 7540 8259 8

British Library Cataloguing in Publication Data available.

Printed and bound in Great Britain by
Antony Rowe Ltd., Chippenham, Wiltshire

One

THE CLANK of the lock and the squeal of the grilled door's hinges filled the cavernous dungeon with dissonant, hollow echoes, rousing Rush Wisdom from a dreamless sleep. He stared drowsily across there, squinting against the glare of two lanterns, his thoughts coming angrily alive as he made out the familiar shapes of the two guards.

They carried shotguns in the bends of their arms and, as one toed a smoking smudge pot in through the doorway, the other bawled, "On your feet, buckos!" having to shout over the mounting ring of chained ankle irons.

Rush Wisdom ran his hands over the dark stubble on his head, over his bare shoulders and chest, brushing off the mosquitos. He stretched his long frame, wincing at the pain in his right ankle that was rubbed raw by a sharp edge of the collar some prison blacksmith had been too shiftless to file smooth. He came tiredly erect then, seeing the shapes of others rising off the floor now, their naked, bony upper bodies agleam with sweat.

This was the Dungeon, the Snake Den, of the Territorial Prison, Yuma, on a summer's eve of the year 1881.

The heat in the vault was a tangible thing, a hot and cottony substance pressing in on a man, filling his lungs, baking his insides. The air was rank, heavy with the sweet-sour smell of unwashed bodies, of filth, and now the acrid stench of the smudge pot's smouldering manure added its rankness to the blend of odors in this big underground room that had been a tomb for so many.

That idle thought, the likening of the granite walled chamber to a tomb, laid a slow tautness along Rush Wisdom's nerves. Reminded of something, he was for a moment unsure of himself. It took a downward glance, a counting of seven grey gouges in the grimy rock beneath the ring bolt and his

1

ankle chains, for him to be absolutely sure. And all at once he was buoyed up, his tiredness and depression gone.

Tonight was the night.

From then on his eyes clung to Jerbaugh, the fat guard. The man was moving his ponderous bulk from one prisoner to another in a too familiar ritual. He would squat heavily, unlock a chain from its ringbolt, a chain that kept its owner apart from his neighbors as he rested, kept him from fighting, sometimes from killing. Drawing the chain from the anklet staples, Jerbaugh would rise and step clear until the freed man was on his way to join those already released facing the other guard's shotgun. He would only then step on to the next man.

A low growl of voices, complaining and edged with scalding hate, was beginning to mount over the steady hum of the mosquitos, its tone muffled and made hollow by the dimensions of the room. And now as Jerbaugh came up to him, not looking him in the eye, Wisdom could ask, "Everything set?" in a normal tone without the risk of being overheard.

Jerbaugh's right eye closed deliberately, the vacuous set of his flaccid face not changing. He stooped and unfastened the padlock. Then, rising suddenly, his shoulder caught Wisdom hard at the ribs, knocking him sharply to one side. The chain caught in its ringbolt and Wisdom was tripped, thrown sprawling.

As he came stiffly to his feet, there were a few raucous guffaws. But the majority of the men hurled obscenities and damnation at the fat guard whose recent brutalities had seemed to make a particular target of but one man, Wisdom.

Finally, the last of the eleven prisoners in line, Jerbaugh came over to stand alongside his companion, his coarse voice grating, "Todd, Lockhart, Bulow and Remick work the graveyard tonight. The rest—"

A snarl from the man alongside Wisdom cut across the guard's words, and there were mutters from another man. Jerbaugh smiled smugly, saying, "Want to go back to workin' daytime, you two? She was a hundred and twenty-seven up there at noon." He waited a moment, letting the threat carry its weight. Then, glancing briefly at Wisdom, he went on, "Lockhart, you're grub tender at midnight. The rest of you go with Meeker here and load garbage first off. All right, out you go!" and he nodded to the door.

Rush Wisdom—known here as Lockhart, the name under which he had been tried and convicted—kept his place in line out along the rock corridor and then up the steps to the outside compound. While they took their turns at the water bucket there, he looked toward the heavens, saw the multitude of winking stars and thought dismally, *Another clear night!* the gloominess of that observation lightened only slightly at sight of the new moon's thin sickle hanging low in the blackness to westward.

The heat out here was worse than below, though drier, not so oppressive. And after he had spilled a dipperful of water over his head, Wisdom was trying to guess the spot Jerbaugh would mark off for the new grave, hoping it would be dug close to the river bluff's edge. Everything from now on depended on Jerbaugh.

Presently they were grouped close beneath the main guard tower along the high wall, and as they were being separated into their two work details Wisdom glanced above and saw another pair of guards, these with rifles, pacing the parapet. He idly wondered with a sober concentration how accurately those two could shoot at night, knowing that the graveyard was within easy range. He would probably have the answer to that one way or the other before the night was out. In fact, it would be proved precisely at midnight, when Jerbaugh sent him for the food buckets.

That thought of food made him aware of the gnawing hunger in him now, a feeling so constant and long endured he hardly noticed it any more. A man's guts shrunk almost to nothing on this midnight and morning schedule for eating. They'd have shrunk even on three meals of the thin potato soup flavored with *chili*, the soggy *tortillas*, and once in a long while the stringy bits of goat meat the Mexican cooks stewed the life out of. Food was the one thing Wisdom wondered about above all the imponderables this particular night promised, for in his four months here he had been plagued by dreams of full, rich meals that sharpened his hunger until he had become like the rest and would steal if his neighbor dared turn from his plate an instant. He hoped he would have food tonight, plenty of it.

Jerbaugh's voice broke across his thoughts now. "Lockhart, lead off!"

Wisdom led the three others out through the main gate, across the road and down the sandstone path toward the cemetery, Jerbaugh's lantern swaying behind and casting their elongated shapes in a grotesque dance before them. Off to the right he could see several lights winking from below among the sorry clutter of the town's 'dobe houses. And from down there floated out across the still, hot night the lilting strumming of a guitar, and the muted ripple of laughing voices, sounds to sharpen a man's loneliness. Yet as they reached the graveyard's rotten granite shelf Wisdom was intent on one thing only. He was looking into the blackness at the far limit of the bluff, the river's edge, fascinated by it, seeing it as a beckoning sanctuary.

Everything depended on Jerbaugh. The guard had played his crafty game for three weeks now, passing the word outside, his stubby fingers rubbing the gold of a double-eagle each time he thought of some further delay. *And it'll be the same tonight, damn him!* came Wisdom's dismal conviction then.

If midnight was the agreed time, then midnight was the hour to avoid. Wisdom was certain of that the instant the notion struck him. There was a near panic in him then as he kept on walking toward the picks and shovels, the jack hammers and pins scattered at this near end of the rubble mound marking the grave they had finished last night. Jerbaugh was to move them to a new spot. He had agreed it would be close to the edge of the bluff. But the man couldn't be trusted to keep his word. He had probably already thought of another reason for further delay.

Now, now's your time! came Wisdom's angry, rebellious thought. *Now, while he's least expecting it.*

He looked furtively around to see Jerbaugh trudging a safe twenty feet behind the last man, watching that man, the shotgun hanging at arm's length, lantern in the other hand. He reached the grave mound and kept straight on, head turned, his eye on the guard. He saw the face of the man immediately behind him go suddenly slack with surprise. He lengthened his stride, feeling the heavy slap of the iron gouging his right ankle bone. A quick glance ahead then showed him the rim of the bluff a bare fifty feet ahead. And all at once, involuntarily, he broke into a hard run.

He was halfway to that beckoning blackness when he saw Jerbaugh's fat bulk halt sharply. The guard set his lantern down and swung the Greener to shoulder all in one wickedly fast move. Wisdom knew that instant he wasn't going to make it.

There was no choice here. Now that he had committed himself, Jerbaugh would shoot regardless. The guard bellowed a shout of alarm as the shotgun settled to his shoulder. Wisdom threw himself in a rolling fall hard to the left.

The Greener's blast threw a thundering echo back from the prison wall the instant Wisdom felt his chest sprayed with stinging rock particles. He hit the ground on one shoulder and rolled. The hot stab of one lead pellet was ripping along his side as he realised Jerbaugh's shot had been too far to the right. He heaved himself on, still rolling to the left in a frantic scrambling he hoped would carry him beyond the lantern's reach. The thunderclap explosion of Jerbaugh's second barrel marked the exact moment he felt himself falling over the rim's edge.

Once again there came the burn of rock dust stinging his flesh, this time his back. He was sliding downward, and he threw his legs around and dug his bare feet into the yielding talus of the bluff's steep face. He kept on sliding for several seconds. Then, with a jarring wrench that buckled his knees, his momentum halted and he surged erect, knowing he was on a narrow shelf some thirty feet below the rim. Carefully now, he took one step, another. His outstretched foot felt the edge then.

It was a simple thing; he'd gone over and over it in his thoughts, this stepping off and falling into the downward blackness. But now he did it a different way than in his imagining, a cool fear of doubt at the river's depth directly below making him take a backward step and then hurl himself as far outward as he could spring.

Falling, he briefly glimpsed a faint light cutting the outward blackness, knowing it must be Jerbaugh's lantern coming to the bluff's edge. Then he remembered to double up, to clasp his knees.

The water slammed his spine with a force that seemed to rip his back muscles apart. The wind was driven from his lungs in a gusty, gurgling exhalation he couldn't control. He felt himself going down. He was gagging, trying not to take a breath as he arched his body straight. His left foot suddenly scraped a sharp edge of rock, settled to a firmer surface. He bent his legs and pushed upward.

That burst to the river's surface carried him chest-high out of the water. He dragged in a deep lungful of air before he went under the second time. He struck out, trying to stay below the surface, and he swam until his chest ached before he pushed upward once more.

His head came out of the water, and he rolled onto his back, looking above trying to orient himself. He had barely glimpsed the high bluff and the lantern shining there when a rosy wink of powder-flame stabbed down at him from the rim's edge. He thrashed his body around and under once more, feeling the bite of buckshot along his legs, hearing more of it slap the water. He threw his head up, took another mouthful of air, went down again, striking out into the current, feeling it catch him in its powerful hold.

When he next came up and looked around, he was a good hundred feet from the bank. The lantern was further away, no longer looming so threateningly overhead. Another shot boomed across the river's dark reach. He didn't bother looking back when it came, nor did he dive again. For he had stretched his chances now until they began to look like something.

He was almost out of the shotgun's range. Instead of being tricked, he had tricked Jerbaugh. He could imagine the insults being hurled at the guard now by the other three prisoners, the confusion and delay they would be working to slow the beginning of the hunt. With tired, slow strokes, he started doggedly across the swift reach of the muddy Colorado.

One thing he hadn't thought out too well was the pull of the current. Off there a hundred yards downstream the starlight let him see the black shadow of the willows where the boat was to be tied. He saw now that he would be swept beyond it, and he tried to put more strength into his strokes.

But the toughness had long ago gone out of him. He felt spent, weak, and for half a minute he lay on his back and did nothing but keep his head above water, trying to gather energy. From then on he forgot the willow thicket and thought only of making the far bank.

Once a distant shouting shuttled across from the direction of the prison. He wondered how long it would take them to lock up the prisoners, to get the dogs out, to wake the ferryman and cross the river. A quarter hour at the most, he guessed.

The river's width had seemed a ridiculously easy swim when he planned this. But now he had to keep crowding back the nagging doubt of being able to make it, and the thought that he might drown. That ominous possibility dampened his relish of being in the water, of its coolness, of his feeling halfway clean for the first time in four months. And finally he was laboring again, spent, struggling as though the water was an enemy trying to drag him down and smother out his life.

Just then he caught a shadow moving across the water from the far shore upstream toward him. He went utterly still, then when he started to sink he moved as little as need be to keep his head up. Gradually that dark shape took on form, became a flat-bottomed boat.

He was struck by another cold doubt, one of Jerbaugh having after all tricked him, of this being a man the guard had posted on the far bank to watch for him and bring him back.

But then a drawling voice shuttled softly over the water. "Rush? That you?" and the vast relief that flowed through him made his voice hoarse as he answered, "Me all right."

The boat came in fast, its shape magnifying quickly in the rush of the current. He lay there feeling a delightful languor settling through him. And then the boat was close, tipping a little as the oars lifted and shed their water in a sibilant, trickling whisper.

"Grab the back," said the man's voice gruffly. He dipped an oar, clumsily brought the stern around, Wisdom all the while studying the stocky, hunched-over shape he was glimpsing for the first time.

One hard stroke put the scow close in as it threatened to glide on past. Wisdom reached up, caught a hold on the gunwale. The craft tipped sluggishly, he shifted his hold on around and gripped the stern with both hands, breathing gustily, "Move along!" And as he felt himself pulled powerfully through the water he forgot his exhaustion long enough to exert a last effort and haul himself up and belly-down across the stern.

He lay there, legs trailing in the water, unable to move a muscle as he gagged for breath. He heard a thumping of the oars against the boat's sides, and abruptly felt a hold at his armpits. He struggled weakly, trying to help as he was pulled into the boat and drew his legs around. The moment he sat on the stern thwart he said weakly, "Keep movin', Idaho."

He sat there with head hanging, dragging in deep lungfuls of air. He felt the boat surge rhythmically as Idaho set to work once more. He felt the sting at his ankle and looked down to see the two black circlets of iron above the pale pattern of his feet. And suddenly a surge of outright delight rose in him and a deep laugh welled up out of his chest. His laughter held on, became louder and took on a note of lunacy.

"Hell, keep it quiet!" grumbled the other's voice, and the rowing stopped.

Wisdom sobered at once, thinking rationally again. He lifted his head and eyed that shadowy, chunky shape ahead, trying to make out the man's face. "So you're Idaho," he breathed. "Never was so glad to meet a man."

"You may be sorry you ever did, friend."

Wisdom's breathing wasn't so labored now, and that feeling of utter exhaustion was slowly draining away as he watched Idaho. The man didn't know how to row at all well, for the scow's square bow kept yawing through a wide arc. He was pulling hard, almost viciously, yet the black shadow of the river's west bank didn't seem to be drawing any closer.

All at once the panic was crowding Wisdom again. He eased forward onto his knees and caught a grip on the oars over Idaho's knotted hands as they swept forward. Even the feeble strength he was able to put against the oars made a difference, and when Idaho grunted, "Quit, you're only in the way!" he told the man sharply, "Like hell!"

They went on that way for almost two minutes, until Wisdom's failing strength made them lose the beat and he had to sit back on his heels and rest. It was then that Idaho said gloatingly, "So you outguessed the polecat! Knew you would."

Wisdom only sat there watching the black shadow of the bank, trying by rocking his body to speed the boat's sluggish onward surge. Idaho was grunting with each stroke, the work beginning to tell on him. And now, from across the black stretch of water behind them, there came the sudden, muted baying of hounds.

Idaho said, "We'll make it, by God!" He took another deep breath, his hard stroke not breaking as he said haltingly, "You got a second jughead . . . staked at water hole over the border . . . Busted-in wickiup at hole . . . due south . . . can't miss it."

Wisdom shook his head. "No. They pay these Indians fifty dollars to bring us back. I'll go north."

Idaho went motionless, letting the oars trail in the water, breathing heavily. Wisdom said quickly, sharply, "Keep at it!" Then, because he sensed the man was about to protest, he went on, "There was a bird back there knows the country. I've got it all in my head, water holes, where to cross the river, everything."

"There's a world of desert off there," Idaho said ominously as he set to work once more.

"So there is. But I'll take my chances."

Wisdom went forward onto his knees again, pushing on the oars. Once they were closing in on the bank sharply, but Idaho pulled hard on the left oar and put them parallel to the bluff, saying shortly, "Further down."

It came to Wisdom then that he owed this man a great deal, perhaps his life. He wanted to tell him exactly that, tell him that when they got in touch with each other later there would be money, lots of money.

But as he was trying to find the words to say what he had in mind, Idaho suddenly drawled, "You're headin' back for Longbow, eh?"

Surprised, Wisdom could only nod.

"Goin' home first?"

Again Wisdom nodded. "It'll be safe enough, since my name never got into it."

Idaho laughed brittlely. "You're a hell of a lot like Frank. He'd've gone back."

His words prompted a new chain of thought in Wisdom that made him ask, "Can you tell me anything at all about Frank? About how he died?"

"Not one damned thing."

Over a short silence, Wisdom softly said, "Then I'll go into it blind. On a high lonesome. I'll get the answers if it takes ten years, twenty."

"And me, I'll be right with you."

Wisdom let his hands fall from the oars. "You?"

"Me. What's to stop me? The price on my head?" The man gave that unamused, sharp laugh again. "Hunh-uh! Frank Wisdom was the one real friend I had left on this earth. Name the day and I'll be right there in Longbow aside you."

There was something to be decided here that Wisdom hesitated over. He owed it to Frank, to Frank's memory, to give this man a chance of sharing his revenge, whatever that was to be. And now, gently, he said, "Friend, I want to square this with you. Whatever it's worth. I'll send it wherever you say."

"Money? Hell, no. All I want's a chance at whoever threw that bullet. You name the day and I'll be there. In Longbow."

Wisdom drew in a deep sigh, it occuring to him then that

having a man like Idaho to side him might after all pay off. And finally he said, "Make it the fifteenth of September, month after next."

"I'll be there."

The high-bodied freight lumbered heavily up the mired grade, its three teams slogging unevenly against the traces, the ring of its double-tree chains and the rattle of brake blocks muted by the murmur of a steady downpour. A thick stand of pines lay to either side of the road, and off to the east grey, leaden clouds shrouded the shoulder of an aspen blanketed ridge. Winter's first bitter chill lay heavy in this high country air.

Rush Wisdom sat the high driver's seat, head tilted to the slant of the rain as, hands under slicker, he worked with tobacco and paper. Shortly he drew out the cigarette and passed it to the driver. "It's yours if you can keep it going."

"If she won't burn, she'll chew." The man dipped his head in thanks, wound the leathers about the brake arm and made his light.

This was early morning of September fifteenth, seven weeks from the night Wisdom had headed into the wilderness north of Yuma. Long days of saddlework and plenty of plain food had brought considerable change in his rangy frame. Many of the forty-odd pounds he'd taken on since that night on the river with Idaho had gone into his shoulders. He was solid, though still slender, and sun and wind had dark-burned the sallowness from his lean face. He had a head of hair again, black hair that was still short but not noticeably so.

It had taken him better than a month to shed one annoying prison habit, a certain ceaseless and wary roving of his deep blue eyes, something he had gradually discovered was pointless once he was among friends again. The prison scars, the visible ones and most of the hidden, had disappeared. That long-gone rawhide toughness, the physical well being, had returned. Outwardly, he was a whole man once more.

But inwardly there was one definite change. He would never be quite the same again, never as carefree and lighthearted as in the old days. The only outward evidence of this was a quiet manner and a look of maturity, one that would prompt a man to place him in his middle thirties rather than in his twenty-eighth year. He was soberly aware of a thin, deep strain of bitterness in his makeup that hadn't been put there by the long, punishing months in Yuma. The bullet that had taken Frank Wisdom between the shoulders had put it there, and he knew he would never rid himself of this unwanted, unnatural emotion till he came face to face with the man who had thrown that bullet.

Time and again over these past weeks he had tried to reckon just what facts he had to go on, and now as the wagon jolted up the rocky road he thought of them again. The most definite of all was the telegram Frank had sent him from Longbow. This had stated obscurely that Frank had run into trouble, that someone had tried to bribe him, that he needed help. Would Rush meet him in Laramie on a certain night, at the stage station? Finally, the message cautioned Rush to travel under the name of Lockhart, as Frank himself was doing.

That warning of using another name hadn't been surprising. Frank Wisdom had been a geologist, well known in his profession, and while on an assignment he had long ago learned the need of keeping his identity hidden, for his work was often of a confidential nature.

So Rush had gone to Laramie using the name Lockhart, arriving there a day early. His arrest had come the second night as he was on his way to meet Frank. They had tried him the following day, after letting him see Frank's body briefly. A man he had never before laid eyes on—a man with a narrow face and shifty, beady eyes—had testified against him, stating he had seen the defendant shoot the deceased, Frank Lockhart, without warning along a side street the previous evening. No, the deceased hadn't been armed. He could identify the defendant positively from having seen him run past a lighted tar barrel in front of a saloon as he made off from the scene of the killing.

The only surprising thing about the trial had been its outcome, the judge's pronouncement of life imprisonment instead of hanging. Rush's plea for a delay so as to summon friends who could help him had counted for nothing. He would have told of using an assumed name, would have given his right one, but for being warned against doing so by the lawyer the court had appointed to defend him, this lawyer insisting it would only heighten the prejudice of the jury against him.

Those were the main facts he had to go on. There were a few more details Idaho had given him as they climbed the

river bluff below Yuma that night to where the horses were
waiting. This man who had been Frank's helper off and on
over the past ten years, who had occasionally worked for Frank
even after being outlawed, had seen Frank only briefly in
Longbow. He had been told of the Laramie trip, of Rush
joining Frank, had been told to wait in Longbow. Frank
hadn't even vaguely mentioned whom he was working for,
what he was doing. It had been three weeks before Idaho had
known what had happened to Frank, and to Rush. Convinced
of Rush's innocence, he had made his slow way across the
thousand miles to Yuma.

All this gave Rush Wisdom pitifully little to go on, or so
he was thinking. Yet, with the wet chill of this high country
air biting into him now, he was warmed by a lively anticipation, by an eagerness to see what this day would bring. He
had never doubted Idaho's being here to meet him, and it
was possible this friend of Frank's had run onto something.
Over these past weeks he had sometimes caught himself
wondering over the particulars backing the law having put a
price on Idaho's head. He could vaguely remember Frank
having mentioned the man's trouble summer before last.
Idaho had evidently killed a man in some trouble over a
woman down in The Nations. Regardless of what the details
might have been, the very fact of Frank having overlooked
them was reassuring, and Wisdom had long ago decided that
he could have picked few better men than Idaho to side him.

A sudden gust whipped along the aisle of the road now,
and he and the driver both tilted their heads further against
the icy spray. It had been like this halfway through a hard
night, all these two hours since dawn. It was a bitter, bleak
day, and as the freight slowly topped the grade, the teams
tiredly picking up the pace, the driver stated with a gusty
relief:—

"Town, by God! She never looked so good!"

Ahead now, Wisdom could see a clutter of sheds around
a barn in a clearing through the timber. A rail fence ran up
along the road between tall lodgepoles turned an emerald-
grey by the rain. There were a few scattered log and slab
cabins in sight beyond the wagon lot, though these and the
driver's comment were all Wisdom had to let him know that
this was Longbow, the end of seventeen days of travel for him.

The driver abruptly reached for the whip and swung it so
that it exploded soddenly between the flanks of the leaders.

The teams lunged to a trot, and when they came up on the gate they were at a dogged, slow run. The driver swung them between the log uprights with a sure recklessness that had the rear wheels sliding across the heavy plank ramp. Then, immediately beyond and alongside a platform and shack, he booted home the brake and leaned against the reins. The blocks screeched and the topheavy Peter Schutler wagon slid to a stop along the slippery planks with the teams loudly snorting a pale vapor against the cold.

Wisdom said, "You have my thanks for the lift, friend," and the driver answered as he swung down to the wheelhub, "Couldn't leave you and the lady stranded back there, could I?"

That moment the door of the gate shack swung open hard to bang against the wall. A man of enormous proportions stepped out onto the platform, having to turn sideways and duck his head as he came through the opening. He had a square, jowled face and his frame was massive, looking only a trifle fat.

He was eyeing the driver with an open hostility as he said in a booming voice, "Midnight it was to be, eh? Man, you're fired!"

Wisdom glanced down to see the driver's face stiff with alarm. "Now listen, Myrick," the man said in a pleading tone. "The road's out part of the way and Crosson's wash was runnin' belly deep to the teams. Barney was bogged down there with a busted axle, on that rise out toward the middle. Was I supposed to let the old coot sit there and drown? Him and his passengers, this gent and a lady? You'd of—"

A hard angry lift of Myrick's hand cut him short. "All right, you get one more chance. Now let's get that freight unloaded in time to catch the haul south for Timberline." ... He scowled as he briefly regarded Wisdom, who was coming aground now ... "Where's Barney? Where's the lady?"

Wisdom started wading the muddy planks toward the wagon's rear as the driver's answer came. "Barney took his teams and the mail to Crosson's place. The lady's back there snug and dry under the tarp."

Myrick came on across the ramp, giving Wisdom a baleful, lowering glance as he saw him unknotting the ropes holding the wagon's canvas in place over the end gate. He strode on in and pushed Wisdom out of the way, shoved him so hard that he nearly lost his footing against the wet planks.

"Easy, mister!" Wisdom drawled.

"Then out o' my way!"

Myrick drew a knife from pocket and unceremoniously cut the rope so that the canvas fell open. Looking up into the wagon then, the black anger all at once left his face. And as he unchained the end gate and let it fall, he was smiling broadly, reaching up to say, "Well, Martha Burke! Ed didn't say it was you. Here, let me give you a hand down."

A young woman, small, slight, stood looking down at him, hesitating. She said uneasily, "I can manage alone, thanks," and knelt in the narrow space behind the bales and crates stacked high under the wagon's tarp.

Myrick gave a throaty laugh and all at once snatched her reaching hand. He pulled her sharply out toward him, catching her under the arms and swinging her around in a surprising show of strength. He stood her on the platform's edge as another would have handled a child, saying, "Always a pleasure to help a lady, Mart."

Color rode into the girl's fair cheeks as she quickly turned from the big man. "I thought you were letting me fall." And the embarrassed glance she gave Wisdom made him think her far prettier than he had judged her by lantern-light at one o'clock this morning.

But then he revised his opinion somewhat. She had an interesting face rather than a pretty one. The mouth was too wide to be in balance with a slender, freckled nose, and there was a prominence of cheekbone that didn't fit the face's oval outline. And now as she hurried over to get out of the rain and stand beneath the shack's sheltering overhang, she wore a sober expression that hinted at a patient resignation and a quiet strength. There was a maturity about her, a womanliness that only now told him she was older than he had thought.

He noted with some relief that her pale hair, the color of oat straw, was dry once more and that she was wearing her hat again. The shoulders of her matching, slender waisted coat no longer showed the dark stains of the night's wetting.

He sauntered across to join her, saying, "See you've managed to dry out a little."

She laughed easily, her grey eyes at once brightening with a friendliness. "Which is more than you can say. Are you as cold and miserable as you have a right to be?"

"Nothin's wrong that a dry outfit and a meal won't cure."

He saw her glance shift suddenly beyond him in the direction of the gate, her expression losing its warmth. Then deliberately, coolly, she was nodding to someone. He turned to
see a poncho draped rider on a leggy chestnut horse wading
the mud of the road just short of the gate, the man in the
act of doffing his hat with an extravagant gesture despite the
misty rain.

That instant there came a thud against the planks close behind Wisdom. The next, a heavy weight struck the back of
his boots. He wheeled sharply around, seeing his sacked saddle
lying there at his feet, seeing the clean lines it had left in
sliding through the ooze and a puddle close by.

His glance whipped across to Myrick in time to catch the
big man heaving his valise this way after the saddle. And the
crunch of the valise as it hit the planks pulled tight a thread
of anger in Wisdom as Martha Burke was saying:—

"Must you always be showing off, Myrick?"

"His stuff's in the way."

Myrick was eyeing Wisdom arrogantly, challengingly as he
spoke. The man's overbearing manner, his smugness, had their
effect on Wisdom. The punishment last night had given him
had played on his nerves. And now that thread of anger
in him snapped, and he started across the ramp straight at the
big man.

When he was three strides away, Myrick squared off at him,
a malicious gleam coming into his close-set eyes. The big man
drew back his right arm deliberately. He swung viciously, fast,
as Wisdom came in.

There was an instant when a wild exultation hit Wisdom,
when he was wondering if he'd be regretting this. Then he
was instinctively rolling his shoulder below Myrick's punch,
shifting his weight with a practiced expertness. He felt
Myrick's fist glance off the point of his shoulder, and he let
the drive of that blow add momentum to a feint with his right
hand, then to the full swing of his left.

He struck for a point beyond Myrick's head with that trick
of the fighter who asks the best of a blow. His fist caught the
big man full on the mouth, the knuckle impact traveling all
the way into his elbow. He saw Myrick's head snap back and
the hat fly from the man's head.

Myrick had counted on that single roundhouse swing to
connect and decide this, for his guard only now was lifting.
And suddenly, with the knowledge he could whip this massive

man, a blind and awful fury blazed in Wisdom. He shifted
his weight fast and threw his right hard after the left.
Myrick saw the blow coming and tried sluggishly to heave
his ponderous bulk to one side. He was too late.

Wisdom's fist smashed at the man's jaw hinge. The bewildered look in Myrick's eyes changed to one of utter
vacancy. He was out on his feet. Wisdom knew that. Yet
some hot, killing instinct drove him to hit again, and still
again, chopping at Myrick's face.

All at once the realization of what he was doing struck
home to Wisdom. Awed by it, he stepped back and let his
hands drop. Myrick's knees had locked. And now he fell to
the muddy planks slowly, like a brick chimney, like a log,
with a certain towering and stately majesty.

Rush Wisdom's chest was heaving as he raised his right
hand and licked the blood from skinned knuckles. He stood
there staring down at Myrick with that wicked fury still
writhing as it slowly died in him. He could scarcely believe
what he had just done. And all at once he was loathing himself for the smallness, the pettiness of this brutal act.

Here was something unexpected, awful, that Yuma had left
with him, a hard and malignant core of fury doubtless nur-
tured by the beatings guards had given him, by the brawls
with fellow prisoners that had sometimes meant the difference
between a man's surviving or his dying. Still, his fury just now
had been pointless, unnecessary. It put a rank taste in his
mouth, it was an alien instinct that made him rebel. And he
was deeply ashamed.

He noticed now that the driver, who had been unhitching
the teams, was standing at the far end of the platform and
had seen all this. For the man's look was one of disbelief,
amazement as he abruptly came on past the wagon and knelt
beside Myrick to say in an awed, hushed way, "He'll be out
for a week!"

Behind Wisdom, the girl spoke lifelessly. "He may have
had that coming. But now you won't dare stay in this town."

When Wisdom looked around at her questioningly, she
went on in a rising voice, "Do you think he'll let it go at this?
He's a brute. He'll come after you again. With anything he
can lay hands on. A club or . . . or maybe even a gun."

A horse's slow hoof falls along the ramp's planks behind
him took Wisdom's attention then. Turning, he found the
rider who had half a minute ago been on his way past the

gate putting the chestnut in alongside the platform. The man had a slender build, and looked to be in his early thirties. He was blond haired, handsome, and just now his face was set in a delighted smile.

As he reined in, the newcomer said, "I shall be the envy of every man in this town. Stranger, that was an unbelievable sight. Allow me to congratulate you."

For a moment Wisdom was at a loss in placing the man's cultured, almost foreign accent. But then he was remembering an Englishman he'd once met at a buffalo camp, and realized that this was the same breed of man.

He nodded civilly and stepped on over to pick up saddle and valise. While his back was still turned, the man said, "It would please me mightily to arrange a match between you and Myrick. We could fill Harkness's warehouse. I would lay money—"

"George, please just let it go!" the girl interrupted. "You know what trouble there'll be without your adding more."

"Trouble, Martha?" ... Wisdom faced around as the man was putting the question ... "Not at all. Anything but. Myrick and this man can settle their differences in a sporting manner, as gentlemen. They can also split a fat purse. And—"

"Not interested," Wisdom cut in. "Forget the whole thing." He glanced at Martha Burke. "You have a way of getting home?"

She nodded, her grey eyes still troubled. "They'll either take me or send for my father. Can I ... I'd like to thank you again for what you did last night."

"We were lucky," Wisdom told her, dipping his head to her and starting on out the platform toward the gate.

Presently, beyond the gate and walking a puddled cinder path flanking the rail fence, he heard a horse coming up behind him. Shortly the man on the chestnut was pulling in alongside him, saying, "Don't be too hasty, my friend. I would guarantee you five hundred dollars if you'd agree to fight Myrick. My name, by the way, is Durwent. George Durwent."

Wisdom put down his rising impatience, looking around at the man with a spare smile. "You're mighty interested. Why?"

"I would manage the bout," came this George Durwent's bland admission. "Last year I matched friend Myrick with a sawyer from a camp near Timberline. We made some money, all three of us."

"Then find another like your sawyer to take on Myrick."

"Who would that be? No, sir. Myrick's too well known around here. This sawyer he licked was in bed for a month."

"Thanks for the warning." Wisdom was finding this man likeable despite his stubbornness. And now, seriously, he added, "But you can count me out. I may be gone from here tomorrow, depending."

"Depending on what?"

Wisdom thought a moment, finally saying, "Work. What else?"

"You'd earn more in one night if you fought Myrick than you could in the saddle over half a year."

"No, thanks."

Durwent had been intent on this argument. But now seeming to sense he was losing by pressing the point, he smiled good naturedly. "All right. You're a man who knows his mind. But if you change it, let me know." Lifting the reins, he added dryly, "And now I'll be on my way to get the doctor." With a friendly nod, he touched spur and put his animal at a heavy run on up the street.

Wisdom kept on along the puddled path, unmindful of the wetting he was giving his boots as he immediately forgot Durwent in the face of the aftermath of that savage wildness that had been in him. It had left him sober, thoughtful, in a way doubting himself; and it was only gradually that he started noticing his surroundings.

He was passing more cabins, an occasional frame house, and up ahead through the pines he could make out the false fronts of two stores, the biggest proclaiming, *Kramer & Son, Dry Goods, Gents Wear, Post Office*, and the other, *Wood Davis, Hardware, Implements, Fencing.*

The street climbed gradually and its ruts were brimming with sluggishly flowing water as he came to a plank walk and strode on under a wooden awning, the rain no longer tapping the shoulders of his poncho: He passed several people, one of them an elderly woman who smiled at him, saying cheerily, "Good morning, sir." He nodded at her, " 'Morning, ma'am" and this pleasant interchange lifted him out of his indrawn, brooding mood, letting him put the fight from mind.

He came even with a saloon's window, read the legend,

Fine and Dandy, lettered on it and couldn't help smiling. A swamper was pushing a dirty, littered pile of sawdust out the swing doors as he passed, and the rank odor of the place lay heavy in the damp air. A saddle shop was immediately beyond. At the walk's outer edge stood a stuffed bay horse on small rollers, its neck arched, the new saddle and bridle it wore studded with nickelwork. Then, up ahead, he made out a sign hanging over the walk, *Eats*, and he hurried on, suddenly realizing that food was what he needed before anything else.

He ordered steak and potatoes and, "Coffee right away," after he had dumped saddle and valise and was shedding his poncho to one side of the door. His need for the coffee made him burn his mouth when the cup was set on the counter before him, and when his plate came he wolfed the food with a relish the restaurant man noted and appreciated.

This was the slack time of the morning, beyond the breakfast hour, and now and then one man, or a pair of men, would come in to have coffee and leave after a brief interval of idle talk. Wisdom paid the customers scant notice, his attention being strictly on his meal.

It was as he was spooning the second cup of coffee to cool it that he heard the door open as it had several times over the past minutes. Then the restaurant man at the front of the room was saying, "A poor day, sheriff."

"Bad as they come, Walt."

One word of the casual interchange laid an instant wariness through Wisdom. Sheriff. Every muscle in him was tightening as he heard the newcomer's step approaching along the counter. It was all he could do to keep from looking around, so strong was his sense of being a hunted man with one of the hunters closing in on him. Rarely was he aware of the weight of the .44 Colt's and shellbelt sagging at his thigh, for they had long ago become as much a part of his dress as boots, shirt or hat. But he was made hard aware of the weapon now as the sheriff's voice spoke suddenly from close behind him:—

"You the one I hear had the go 'round with Myrick?"

Wisdom turned slowly around, schooling his expression to impassiveness as his glance started lifting along this man's lank length. He drawled, "I am."

What he saw then brought him strong surprise. This sheriff was as unlike a law man as any he had ever laid eyes on. No badge was visible on the coarse woolen shirt under the open coat. No gun hung along the lean thigh, nor was there the bulge of one below the coat's shoulder. The early middle-aged look of this man's thin, hawkish face made a sharp contrast with his silver hair. His appearance might have labelled him as being a cattleman, the hard working owner of a small brand.

But it was the eyes that were hardest for Wisdom to understand. A deep brown, their sober regard now abruptly broke before a look that was surprisingly friendly; and they no longer belonged to a peace officer. A slow smile rode over the man's face then to give it an almost youthful cast and flatten the line of its wide, blond moustaches.

"Can't help bein' just as pleased as the next man over this," the sheriff stated. "So we'll forget the lecture I came to read you, stranger. Myrick's still alive, which is my only lookout for now. A lot of folks will be wanting to buy you a drink for—"

"John, looks like trouble across there!" came a call from the restaurant man, cutting short the other's words.

The sheriff turned, glancing toward the street. And Wisdom, the apprehension in him slowly easing away, looked on out the window to see a group of perhaps a dozen men coming along the far walk. They were keeping pace with three horses wading the mud close to the opposite rails. Two of the animals carried riders shrouded in shapeless, dark slickers. The third was packed with some bulky object covered by a grimy canvas.

"Isn't that Ann on the bay?" the sheriff asked in a startled way.

"Looks like her." The restaurant owner followed his sober words by asking gloomily, "Wonder who the unlucky one is?"

The sheriff shrugged. And it was only then that Wisdom noticed a boot swinging stiffly below the edge of canvas along the lead pony's barrel across there and understood what had alarmed these two.

"A poor day to pick for dyin'," the sheriff observed quietly as he glanced around at Wisdom again. His soberness held on them as he asked, "You're to be here a while, stranger?"

Wisdom gave much the same answer he'd given Durwent a quarter hour ago. "Depends on what luck I have findin' work."

"You won't have much, not this time of year." Mildly, the

law man went on, "You're not askin' advice, but let me offer some. Ray Myrick's the kind that would twist a youngster's arm for the fun of hearin' him yell. Keep an eye out for him."

"I'll do that, sheriff."

"Another thing. I wouldn't . . ." Breaking off his words, the sheriff's glance took on a definite shyness. He lifted his bony shoulders then, saying, "Hell, I talk too much with my mouth! Just you be careful is all. We want no gunplay over this." And with a spare nod he headed for the street.

As the door slammed behind the man, Wisdom let his breath go in a gusty, worried sigh. He had spent considerable time over these past weeks planning how, as a wanted man, he was to remain inconspicuous in the eyes of whatever law he found in Longbow. Now all that careful consideration had been wasted. Had he deliberately set about attracting the law's attention, he could have settled on no surer way than in fighting Myrick. He had only his stupidity, and that strange and uncontrollable fury, to blame for having put himself in a position that was the last he would have chosen. He would have to be very careful from here on out, for this likeable sheriff couldn't help but be curious about him.

He watched the law man stepping to the walk's edge now, and saw that one of the riders was angling his way across the street. He had forgotten the sheriff's surprised query of a minute ago until this moment as he caught a profusion of deep chestnut hair showing below the line of the approaching rider's hat. He paid a stricter attention then, and shortly the girl was close enough to give him the strong impression that her looks were uncommonly striking.

He kept his glance on her through the dusty window as he went to the front of the room and laid a dollar on the counter saying, "Good meal."

The restaurant man nodded, making change as he looked out onto the street and dryly remarked, "Fine chore to be wishin' on a woman."

"Who is she?"

"Daughter to Matt Ladd, poor devil."

"Poor because he's got her for a daughter?"

"Not on your life! Poor because he's laid up with a bad heart." Wisdom noticed the man's frown as he glanced at the group across the way. "Now what's the sense of that sour damn' Jesse Ober cuttin' Ann in on a deal like this? Cromer ought to call him on it."

"I don't follow," Wisdom said. "Who's Jesse Ober? And Cromer?"

"John Cromer's sheriff, the one you was just talkin' to. Ober's the one packin' the body. The lonesomest, thievin' son this side the Missouri."

Wisdom crossed to the other side of the door, pulled on his slicker and heaved the saddle to his shoulder. As he picked up the valise he looked out the window once more to see that George Durwent had appeared from downstreet and was joining the girl, who was holding her horse beyond the near rail as she talked to Cromer.

Wisdom was aware of the girl's good looks. She was striking in a way a man seldom saw, and now as she gestured in saying something to the sheriff the motion of her hand was quite graceful. She looked around at Durwent then, and afterward lifted rein and put her horse alongside his, starting up the street with Cromer going on along the walk abreast the two of them.

Wisdom went to the door, asking, "Where's a place for a man to get a room close by?"

"Hotel across the way there above the courthouse." The restaurant man came across to hold the door open. "Ask George for number eight. Lets you see onto the street. Tell him Walt Heffran sent you."

Wisdom said, "Much obliged," as he went out onto the walk, hefting the saddle higher on his shoulder.

He started on after Cromer, the girl and Durwent, who were some thirty feet ahead of him. And shortly he could hear the girl speaking, could catch most of her words. ". . . below those rapids at the foot of Spruce . . . the place, John, there where the river flattens out. He was lying in the deep water against a . . . high at the trail side."

"If the road's caved, the shoring must've given way."

"Not that those timbers haven't been rotten for years."

Wisdom liked the tone of her voice, and the manner of her speaking. She talked as a man would, using words a man would choose, and her voice had a low, rich quality.

She must have noticed him just then, for abruptly she was looking back this way. Her glance touched him casually, went on past him. But then her eyes swung back to him and at once showed an open curiosity that was almost surprise. And in the brief moment their glances held, Wisdom sensed that she became as aware of him as he had been of her. Then Durwent was saying something to her, and with the faintest of smiles she looked away.

When he came to the intersection where a cross street cut the main one, Wisdom angled obliquely through the mire to the far walk, pausing ankle deep in the mud briefly as a buckboard and team splashed past. A light, misty rain pelted his hat and shoulders, and as he stamped the mud from his boots and followed the swelling crowd beyond the cross street he made out a sign bearing the legend, *Exchange*, hanging in front of a broad veranda beyond a two-story brick building halfway the length of the block.

The crowd was well ahead of him, and it wasn't until he stopped further on and was shifting the heavy saddle to his other shoulder that he noticed the increasing throng slowing just short of the brick building. Durwent, Cromer and the girl were crossing toward the waiting crowd now, and he hurried on, knowing then that this must be the courthouse, wanting to pass it before the walk was jammed.

He didn't quite manage that. He was partway through the crowd when three men who had been unleashing the pack animal's burden lifted it down and started for the walk. The crowd shifted, spreading to fill the walk and block his way.

Wisdom stopped, stood watching, his glance idly going to the man who had come in with the girl. This Jesse Ober had stayed in the saddle, and as Wisdom looked at him, thinking how roughly Walt Heffran's tongue had used him, Ober looked this way.

Sight of the man's narrow face jolted Wisdom so hard that he let the warbag fall to the planks. Stark wonderment, then a blazing rage rose in him. Across his mind's eye there flashed a vision of the courtroom in Laramie, of this same man sitting the witness chair solemnly wording the falsehoods that had sent him to Yuma.

Abruptly, Wisdom saw recognition and an expression akin to fear come to this Jesse Ober's eyes as their glances met. He slowly lowered the saddle to the walk, a strange calmness settling through him as he thought of the .44 for the second time today. It occurred to him then that his hunt for Frank's killer had turned out to be ridiculously easy.

Sheriff John Cromer stepped across his line of vision that instant. Sight of the man arrested the move his right hand was making to unbuckle the slicker. And instantly he was thinking again of Yuma, remembering that the law now had a double indictment against him. And that cool, fierce urge to kill slowly left him.

A moment later he was seeing Ober rein his animal out from the tie rail, hearing him call, "Cromer, I got to be gettin' on."

"Better hang around, Jesse." The sheriff was eyeing the man from the walk. "We'll hold the inquest right away."

"I'll be back," Ober called. "Or let the girl tell it. She knows more'n I do." And without further ceremony he started his animal on up the street.

Wisdom was reaching out, intending to put a hold on the arm of the nearest man and ask about Ober, when a wary instinct halted him. Any questions he had about Ober might be held against him later if anything happened to the man. And with a disheartening sense of futility and disappointment he forced himself to begin thinking of what lay ahead, of how he must hunt the man down, settle his score with him and then somehow manage to get out of the country without being seen or missed by anyone.

The three men carrying the body now lugged it awkwardly under the rail and up onto the walk. Wisdom heard Cromer call, "Make way there!" and the crowd shifted further back, blocking the walk more solidly.

Wisdom was watching Ober turn out of sight along a second cross street above the hotel when abruptly he glimpsed the girl bringing her bay to the rail alongside Durwent's horse and the pack animal. He sensed that she had purposely lingered on the street, for the Englishman was already on the walk. And now, still hesitating to leave the saddle, she looked this way over the heads of the crowd, her glance seeming to single Wisdom out.

Once again he was aware of that live curiosity in her regard, of a straightforward and unwavering interest. And now that she was closer, he thrust his thoughts of Ober far enough aside to realize that this Ann Ladd was indeed striking. Her eyes must be light hazel, he decided. The delicacy of her features, finely molded, was subdued by the tan of her complexion. The face was strong, subtly vivacious.

"Leave us through!" someone said testily, and the man ahead of Wisdom backed into him, taking his attention.

The trio carrying the body were quite close now. With

only the faintest curiosity, his thoughts somber and indrawn, Wisdom glanced past the man ahead and down at the grimy canvas. It had come loose, its top fold had fallen back, and he glimpsed the sodden black tangle of the dead man's head.

Then, as the body was being carried past, he could see the face inside the tarp. And cold shock turned him rigid.

The face was Idaho's.

Two

ANN LADD, sitting her horse beyond the rail, caught the slackness that all at once loosened the tall stranger's lean face as he peered down at the body. Wondering at his reaction, not wanting to believe its meaning, it was with an odd sense of disappointment that she finally admitted to herself he must have known Black, this rider of Ober's who had died in the river.

She wasted no love on Jesse Ober or any of the shifty lot who hung around his isolated hill layout. They were men who did most of their riding by night, men who would rein off a trail if they saw you coming, as Ober himself had cut into the timber and tried to circle there at the foot of Spruce Ridge this morning before she hailed him.

She noticed George Durwent now, waiting on the walk for her. Yet as she stepped down into the mud and started his way, her thoughts were still of the stranger. She was hoping he wouldn't turn out to be another like Ober and his kind, like Black; the possibility depressed her without her quite knowing why.

The look she gave Durwent then must have mirrored that depression, for he asked, "Tired, Ann?" as she came across to him.

"No. Do I look it?"

"My imagination," he said relievedly. "No one ever looked better."

She was glancing up at Durwent, purposely ignoring the stranger as they crossed the walk. Yet they were no sooner on the courthouse's narrow portico than curiosity got the better of her, and she looked around to see Wisdom standing there in the scattering crowd, his expression tight-set as though in outrage or pain.

Durwent took her arm now, and she finally gave him her

full attention, pressing her elbow against his touch, telling him, "If I were a man I'd want a stiff whiskey right now, George."

"Let's see if John has some."

She smiled, the idea reviving her naturally good spirits. She glanced down the dusty, gloomy hallway to see Cromer waiting for them by his office door. "Let's," she said, her expression taking on a mock seriousness as they approached the law man. "John, do you keep a bottle in your desk?" she asked. "I need a drink."

It was typical of John Cromer to look less surprised than worried. "None in here. But I can send out for some." He caught the mischievousness in her eyes then and breathed gustily, "Brat!" pushing the door open, unable to hold back a smile before the merriment of her low laughter.

As always when she entered this room, the place struck Ann Ladd as being friendly, like Cromer himself, quite at odds with its function of a law sanctuary. A faded red rug covered the scuffed floor on the window side, a shaded lamp cast a cheery glow over the flat, cluttered desk there. Best of all just now was a feebly flickering blaze in the corner fireplace. The room felt deliciously warm after her cold, wet ride. There was a fragrance in the air, a blend of tobacco and wood smoke, and as she was unbuckling her slicker, letting Durwent help her off with it, she glanced around at Cromer to say:—

"Why can't dad smoke what you do, John? His room sometimes drives you out."

"Make him keep his pipes clean," was Cromer's short answer. "How is he this morning?"

"Cigars, not pipes, John. You really do have your mind on other things." Then she added more soberly, "He seems better. Crosser anyway. That tonic is helping. I'm in for more of it this morning."

Cromer pulled the room's only rocker across from the window to the fireplace now. "Here, sit," he said gruffly. "Get those boots off." And he began laying more wood on the burned-down embers.

As she took the chair, Ann was remembering something. She looked around at Durwent, and the invitation in her eyes at once brought him across to her. He gave Cromer a quick glance, making sure the man's back was turned, then leaned down to kiss her lightly on the forehead.

She looked up at him in a wondering way. Then abruptly she reached up, took a hold on the front of his cowhide coat and pulled him down to her again. She kissed him full on the lips, afterward saying. "Never peck at me, George. You might as well learn that in the beginning."

Cromer had turned and seen this last. And now the ruddiness of Durwent's face deepened. He laughed uneasily, though his, "To think how hard it was getting the first one!" sounded as he intended it should, full of a wry, casual humor.

The sheriff ended that awkward moment by asking, "George, how about gettin' out there by the door, keepin' everyone out? And you might hold onto eight or ten good men to sit the inquest. Leatherwood will want to get it over with right away."

Durwent nodded and at once left the room, the girl meantime weighing the faint edge to the sheriff's words, sensing as she had long ago that John Cromer wasn't overly fond of the man she had chosen. She leaned down now to pull off her boots, not wanting this man who was so like an older brother to her to sense her awareness of his dislike. His opinion of Durwent mattered a great deal, for some of her earliest recollections were of John Cromer as a young wrangler at Brush, her favorite of all the crew. He had taught her much of what she knew of horses and men. Until three years ago he had been her father's foreman, forsaking the job only after Matt Ladd had persuaded him to run for public office.

She was thankful now as Cromer asked tartly, "How come Jesse Ober was with you, kid? And what's he got to say about Black cashin' in this way?"

"He was with me because I stopped him when I saw him sliding around me through the brush right after I came across the body. He took over then. He's sure you'll think it was queer, his happening along when he did. Because he says it looks like he'd been waiting around for someone to find Black."

"The man's thinking is as forked as everything else about him," Cromer stated dryly. "What else did he say about Black?"

"Only one more thing. And it'll interest you." She saw his look turn more alert. "He was coming in today to see you about Black. For some reason he'd become suspicious of him."

"Why suspicious?"

"I didn't ask." ... She leaned over, holding her hands to the leaping flames ... "Jesse Ober's suspicions don't interest me." She glanced around then, surprising Cromer with a wary, eager expression on his face. "Just what does that look mean, John?"

He started to shrug the question aside. Then, with a sudden change of mind, he told her, "All right, if you have to know. It means Ober's right for once. This man's name wasn't Black any more than mine's White. I've known it for a week now and was only waiting to get a line on him. There's a notice in my desk that's got him pegged."

Over her strong surprise, she asked, "He was an outlaw?"

"He was. They wanted him down in The Nations for killing a man in some wrangle over a woman. He's wanted other places for other things. Called himself Idaho. The notice didn't mention a last name."

Once again that mischievousness flared in the girl's eyes. "So you've turned bounty hunter?"

He snorted, not even bothering to deny the accusation. But the next moment he was saying worriedly, "He was around this country a few days this spring, then dropped out of sight. I happened to spot him the night he hit town. Came in by stage. There was a man taking the same stage out that night for Junction. Man by the name of Lockhart. This Idaho and Lockhart had some talk before the stage left. They didn't know I saw 'em."

When Cromer paused, frowning, trying to choose his next words, Ann asked, "Is that anything to be worried about?"

"Wait'll you hear the rest," he told her. "I'd met this Lockhart when he came here to the office with a letter from some railroad. He didn't state what his business was, never told me why he was in the country. Just wanted to meet the law 'In case', he said. When I asked him in case of what, all he'd tell me was I might find out later. And I did."

"You did?"

Cromer nodded soberly. "Lockhart was killed down in Laramie four nights after he left here. Shot in the back. If I hadn't spotted Idaho here the day it happened, he'd have been a good one to bet on having done it. As it turned out, they picked up a brother of Lockhart's down there and sent him up for the murder. Gave him life imprisonment, shipped him to some prison outside the territory because ours was full. Yuma, I think it was."

"Is that still anything to worry about, John?" the girl asked quietly.

"Maybe so." Cromer was on the point then of telling her that the railroad's letter had said their man was working under an assumed name, that his real name was Wisdom. Then, and today as Myrick's driver told him this stranger's name, were the only two times he'd ever run across the name Wisdom. He couldn't disassociate the two.

John Cromer realized now that he was violating one of his strict principles in betraying the confidences of his office, and he went on, "Then again, maybe not. But when a man like this Lockhart sides an outlaw like Idaho, then winds up dyin' the way he did, it makes a man wonder."

"Wonder what?"

"How Lockhart happened to know trash like this killer. Why they were together here. Why Idaho ever came back. There must be reasons."

Ann sat looking up at him, waiting for more. When it didn't come, she said, "Now they're both dead and you'll never get your answers, will you?"

The sheriff shook his head in a baffled way. "Suppose not." He glanced down at her boots on the hearth. "You warm enough by now, kid?" When she nodded, he said, "Then let's hike on into the courtroom and get this inquest over with."

He had crossed to the door and was standing there waiting while she pulled on her boots when abruptly she looked around at him. "John, I noticed a stranger out there. Must've been in Walt's place when you were. Tall, with the deepest blue eyes I've ever—"

His nod cut her short. "The one that beat up on Myrick."

She straightened in the chair, her last boot only halfway on. "Did what?" she asked incredulously.

"What I said. Whipped Ray Myrick."

"No!" Still eyeing Cromer in amazement, she finished pulling on the boot, then rose from the chair and came across to him. "Who is he?"

Cromer opened the door for her. "Goes by the name of Wisdom. I followed him into Walt's to make sure he hadn't bought into trouble he couldn't handle. When I met him I decided he could handle about anything that came along."

He noticed her expression now, the live curiosity that was almost a delight in her eyes. And he said owlishly, "George knows him if you're interested in makin' his acquaintance."

Color came to her cheeks, and as she stepped wordlessly into the hall where Durwent waited, Cromer chuckled softly in the knowledge that for once he had this girl tongue-tied.

George Durwent left town right after the inquest and rode in on his small hill ranch shortly after noon. He was in an unnaturally sober mood and was abrupt with Ira, his colored man and only crewman, who came to take care of his horse.

He walked straight to the house and into his bedroom, locking the door. He pulled a rawhide-bound chest from beneath the bed and squatted on the floor in front of it. The chest contained for the most part personal items having to do with a way of life Durwent would never see again. Chief among these was a bright red Guard's coat, a reminder of debts and scandal. He would have rid himself of the coat long ago but for the stubbornly sentimental belief that it would one day cease to bring back all the unpleasantness and remind him only of the exceedingly pleasant, of the glitter of ballroom nights, of a certain heavily draped box at the Drury Lane, and of concerts and high teas at Kew and Hampton Court.

But now he scarcely noticed anything in the chest as he took a thin ebony letter opener and ran its blade carefully down inside a split along the upper edge of the chest's velvet lining.

Shortly he drew out a single sheet of fine paper with an engraved letterhead, *Railways Limited, Philadelphia, U. S. A.* The page bore a date of seven months ago and read:—

Dear George: Good tidings this time rather than the usual duns of tradesmen, etc. As you probably do not know, this organization has a strong financial interest in the California and Northwestern, the railway that serves your part of the world. Quite recently I have learned that the C.&N. had allotted a considerable sum for the exploration and development of new coal deposits along the Junction division of its line.

You at one time mentioned Junction as being the closest point to Longbow the railway reached, which is why I am giving you the above confidential information.

Now it has occurred to me that perhaps you may know of a source for coal in this region. Also that you might possibly mend your distressed finances by investing in such lands prior to their owners' knowledge of their worth, for the railway will pay handsomely for this coal.

By discreet inquiry I have learned that the C.&N. is next month sending a well known western geologist, a certain Frank L. Wisdom, into your country for the purpose of determining which source of available coal is most suitable to the railway's need. Undoubtedly a rail spur would have to be constructed to this source, so you have the prospect not only of investing in any likely coal deposits but also of buying land along the spur right of way and thus profiting in two directions.

To keep this development completely obscure until the propitious moment, Mr. Wisdom will be visiting Junction incognito under the name of Frank Lockhart. You are to use the utmost discretion in any contact you may have with "Mr. Lockhart," for the obvious reason of not compromising me. I am, sir, your devoted brother.

Alfred.

Although Durwent had remembered the contents of the letter fairly well, he had felt the need of being absolutely certain of the name Wisdom. Six months ago in Laramie, Lockhart was the only name he'd associated with that other Wisdom. And now he saw that it was his bad fortune, rather than the good fortune he'd always considered it, not to have attended the trial and had the testimony of his own eyes to back Jesse Ober's certainty that this newcomer, this Rush Wisdom, was Frank Lockhart's brother.

Ober had furtively sought him out two hours ago after the inquest to give him this sobering word about the stranger who had whipped Ray Myrick this morning. He'd argued with Ober, pointing out that it was up to Ober to take care of himself in this, that the sooner he could do so the less chance he ran of having his false testimony at the Laramie trial come to light. Ober had argued the unfairness of this reasoning, until Durwent reminded him he'd been paid, and paid well, for the Laramie affair.

Now, shoving the chest back under the bed and once more brooding on the inconsistencies of fate, Durwent mused aloud:—

"Well, this time it ought to stick."

Rush Wisdom, an hour out of Longbow, climbed his hired horse along the road below Matt Ladd's pasture fence toward the end of the afternoon, riding in the day's first blaze of strong sunlight. White clouds still lay puffy and spotted all across the down country out of which he had ridden, but ahead the lifting shoulder of an aspen-mantled peak rose into a clean blue sky. The back of the storm had broken.

He was taking his time, wanting to be close below a pass to the northwest at the hour of dusk. A bedroll was tied to his saddle, he had paid the hotel for the next week. He would be the owner of this roan horse but for the livery owner having asked double the animal's worth; and this fact alone, his having bridled over being trimmed on a horse, was his only worry now, the only flaw in his plan.

For he had every intention of keeping on across the hills, of never coming back this way. Jesse Ober's layout was up there near the pass, and whether it took only an hour, or ten days, he was going to settle with Ober and then leave the country by way of the far slope.

This interval since leaving town had only deepened his depression, had confounded him further over the strangeness of Idaho's death. He had attended the inquest, and what he learned there had made him stop for several minutes at the river crossing three miles back along the road. What he had found there at the foot of Spruce Ridge had jolted him, brought him face to face with the stark possibility of Idaho having gone the same way Frank had. And that urge to destroy Ober, strong enough since morning, had grown stronger.

Now, coming to a lane that led toward the big log house sprawling against a backdrop of pines a quarter mile above, Wisdom abruptly drew rein, considering something that hadn't yet occurred to him. From what the liveryman in town had told him, this had to be the Ladd place. He was remembering the girl, the fact that she had been the one who found Idaho's body. And suddenly he was wondering if she could answer any of his questions about the way Idaho had died.

He considered the thing deliberately, his going up there and having a talk with her. There was the remote chance that her answers might sway him into giving up this taking of the law into his own hands, might let him go straight to the sheriff with proof of Ober being Idaho's killer. If he could get that far, he was willing to risk Ober identifying him. If he did get that far, seeing Ober under arrest for murder, he and Cromer might somehow pry from the man the truth about what had happened in Laramie. Here was a slender chance that probably wouldn't pay off. But it was worth taking, and that thought made him put the roan on up the lane.

His somber mood of the past hours lightened a little now as he felt the warmth of the sun on his back. For the first time since early morning, the bone-deep chill that was both physical and mental began thawing out of him. He realized then that this was the kind of bracing afternoon a man long remembered. The air was crisp, heavily laden with the rank smells of new washed earth, of sun-cured grass and pine. And as he scanned the far reaches of the lower hill crests he wondered if he had ever looked upon a fairer country. He was thinking, too, that a man could thrash things around in his mind only so long before he had to do something about it. Whatever was to happen over these next few hours, he was going to do something about Ober one way or the other.

He began paying the layout ahead a critical attention, and shortly gave what he saw his full approval. Ladd's Brush headquarters gave promise of being not only a workmanlike layout but one pleasing to the eye. The rambling log house with its rock foundations and chimneys was big, the varying degree of newness in its timbers clearly showing it had grown from a modest beginning. It looked southwest over half a thousand square miles of fine cattle country. The size of the barns, sheds and corrals sprawling several hundred yards to the east of the house marked it as being a really big outfit.

When he reached a fork in the lane, Wisdom took the one leading in the direction of the house. For two hundred yards he rode along an aisle through pines. He was beyond the trees, taking the grassy incline toward the house, when he glanced toward the wide middle porch and was startled to see Ann Ladd sitting on the steps leading to it.

She was watching him, evidently had been for some minutes. Over his awareness of this, he noticed that she was more slender, more slim-hipped than he'd realized now that he was seeing her in waist overalls and a dark red wool shirt open at the throat instead of the slicker she had worn during the inquest in the chilly courtroom.

She sat with legs outstretched, boots crossed, leaning back with elbows braced on the step above. And as he walked the roan in on the rail at the foot of the steps, he saw that the sunlight laid coppery highlights across her chestnut hair and brought into sharp focus the strong molding of her fine features. She had a beauty that arrested a man's attention, that made him want to keep his eyes on her.

He drew rein and was about to step aground when he first sensed the seriousness of her regard. As he hesitated, there was no break in her gravity. At length, weighing the reserve in her eyes and not at all understanding it, he drawled, "Do I get asked down? Or do I turn and go back?"

It was several seconds before her sober, quiet answer came. "I'm trying to decide."

Her bluntness was unsettling, and over his surprise Wisdom drawled, "There's usually a reason why someone can't stand the sight of me. What's yours?"

"There are several."

He waited, uneasily trying to get some inkling from her look as to how he might be offending. But her eyes told him nothing. There was no particular dislike in them, in fact there was nothing he could define beyond a grave speculation. And finally he asked, "Do I get to know your reasons?"

Her shoulders lifted in a spare shrug that drew the shirt tighter across her gently rounded breasts. "Why not?" she answered in an almost pensive way. "For one thing, there's your knowing Black."

A high wariness at once thrust aside his growing physical awareness of this striking girl as he realized she was leading straight to the point of his being here. "Did I know Black?" he asked.

"You needn't pretend, Wisdom." Her statement was matter-of-fact, showing him no more of her thoughts than he was betraying of his. "I saw the look on your face when they carried him past you into the courthouse."

He shook his head in what he hoped was convincing wonderment. But she didn't wait for him to deny her accusation, saying, "And I think you know Jesse Ober. At least you seemed to. Which doesn't make you welcome here."

"Didn't I see you siding this Ober down the street earlier?" Wisdom asked, lifting a boot from stirrup, sitting the saddle crookedly as he put a forearm against the horn.

"Only because I had to," the girl coolly told him. She was studying him closely then as she added, "One more thing. On the way home I happened to look back from the top of the river ridge. You were down there prowling around the place I mentioned at the inquest, the place where Black drowned. I watched you for all of five minutes. You were still there when I went on."

"So I was," Wisdom admitted. "Tryin' to understand how a man could've fallen from where the trail was caved, then been carried out of the rapids and along to the foot of that quiet stretch below where you say you found Black."

That indrawn quality in the girl's look quickly faded now, her eyes showing a livening interest. She pushed away from the step above. "It is where we found him. But go on."

"You couldn't float a watermelon through those boulders and brush jams at the head of that pool, let alone a body."

She was silent a moment, taking this in. Then she asked "So?"

"So this man was carried as far up from the foot of the trail drop-off as a horse can wade before the pool gets too deep. He was dumped there, a good hundred feet below where he should've been to make it look right."

Wisdom sensed her strong surprise even before she asked, low-voiced, "You're trying to say it was no accident?"

"You decide. Your medico claimed at the inquest it was a fall onto the rocks put the dent in Black's skull. You can decide on that, too."

"What is there to decide on that?"

"Whether it was a rock or something else."

Her hazel eyes came wider open, fixing him with an incredulous stare. "What are you trying to say, Wisdom?"

He lifted his broad shoulders, let them fall. "That other things besides rock will bust a man's head open. The barrel of a Colt's, for one. Or the handle. Or just a plain club."

Abruptly then, from inside the house, came a man's deep voice calling, "Who's there, Sis?"

The girl turned her head to answer. "No one you know, dad."

"Bring him on in anyway!"

"Not just now." She eyed Wisdom once more, the incredulity not gone from her glance. "You did know Black, didn't you?"

He drew in a deep sigh, saying, "I hit a strange town and have a dead man lugged past me. For want of something better to do, I sit in on his inquest. Then—"

"Then you went straight to the river to see how Black died," she interrupted.

Wisdom had a thought then that made him answer, "Sure I was at the river. But I wouldn't've stopped if it hadn't hit me between the eyes how wrong you all are guessin'. Can't you forgive a man a natural curiosity? As for comin' up by way of the river, it's the only way here."

"Here? You were coming here?" When he nodded, she asked, "Why?"

"After a job."

She smiled knowingly then. "Didn't they tell you in town we aren't hiring?"

"They did. But when a man's after work he keeps tryin'."

"Well, you've had your ride for nothing." Ann Ladd's glance had again taken on that speculative, grave quality as she asked, "Are you going to the sheriff with what you know?"

"Why should I? It's not my lookout."

"Then I'll go to him."

"Suit yourself."

She was silent a brief moment, weighing some thought before she stated, "I don't believe a word of your coming here for work. Nor of your not knowing Black. Or Idaho, as the reward notice calls him."

"Your privilege, miss." Once again Wisdom was finding it difficult to hide his strong surprise.

"Ann, bring him in here, whoever he is!"

The coolness that had edged Wisdom's tone made the girl ignore her father's call now. "I didn't mean that exactly the way it sounded," she said in a puzzling about-face. "I apologize."

He smiled thinly, touching his hat to her as he straightened in the saddle and lifted rein, about to turn from the rail.

"Sis, damn it, I say to bring him in!"

The girl looked across at Wisdom then with the first definite break in her reserve. She smiled in a genuinely friendly way, tilting her head toward the porch door, saying,

"It sounds like he really means it. He's sick, and he's lone-some and cranky. He would really like to say hello to you."

"Some other time," Wisdom told her.

"Please do come in."

Her unfeigned humility made this an invitation Wisdom could scarcely ignore. He decided that five minutes more or less didn't matter, and he nodded. Then, as he was swinging his tall frame from the saddle, the girl called, "We're coming!"

Wisdom was on his way up the steps when she told him, "There really is no work for you here. And if Jesse Ober offers you a job, don't take it. He isn't your kind."

"Thanks for that much," he drawled.

She sensed the rebuke, and her face took on a deeper color. "I suppose I had that coming to me. But I mean it, Wisdom. You're not Ober's kind."

"If he's short a man with Black gone, I'm not proud."

"I doubt that Black was at Anchor for any other reason than because it's a good place to hide out. He hadn't been here long."

Here was more information Wisdom had hoped to get from the girl. He was wondering if there was anything else she could tell him about Idaho when abruptly her glance went on past him toward the roan, and she asked, "You aren't buying that horse of Ned Arnholt, are you?"

Wisdom looked down at the animal. "Thought I might. Arnholt claims he's sound."

"Sound, yes. But he's cow hocked, and he's jumpy after dark. I've already warned a friend of mine against him. Now if you need a good animal, we have a mare for sale that can take you places this jughead won't."

For the second time today he was made sharply aware of an unexpected facet to this girl's nature. She was capable in the way expected of a man, and it oddly pleased him to find her so feminine and at the same time so knowing in matters few women ever understood.

But there was another thing he wanted to know about her, a thing that was important to him. And now, standing directly below her, he looked up holding back a smile but letting her see the faintest trace of it. "A lady horse trader," he drawled. "Never ran across one before."

"I'm not a horse trader. I was only trying to help." She spoke aloofly, and turned away across the porch.

"Sure," he agreed with a studied solemnity. "That's part of the trade, tryin' to help a man."

She wheeled suddenly on him, anger blazing in her eyes. But then she read the amusement in his glance and just as suddenly burst out laughing.

"All right, the mare's not for sale then," she told him, and he liked the merriness of her look as she added, "We'll let one of the town sharps give you a real trimming." And she went on across to the door.

This was what Wisdom had been trying to glimpse, this high spirit and quick sense of humor underlying that seriousness she had shown him these past minutes. It had take his baiting to bring this lightheartedness to the surface, and now as he followed her to the door, taking off his hat, he was wondering what instinct had made him so certain it was there.

His first impression on entering the house's main room was one of lightness and color. The furnishings were sturdy, comfortable, the kind that would suit a man, relieved of heaviness and drabness by deft feminine touches, like the lace curtains at the windows and the brightly colored saddle blankets and Indian woven rugs spotted over the broad expanse of pegged floor. It was a pleasing room, with one broad window at the rear giving an awesome vista of the piney mountainside to the north.

Ann Ladd led the way to a door on the far side of a broad fire-place along the left wall, and entered the room beyond saying, "It's the man I was telling you about, dad. Wisdom, the one Myrick had the luck to stub his toe on this morning."

Following her through the doorway, Wisdom's arm lightly brushed against her. And for an instant his awareness was centered wholly upon her nearness, on discovering how much taller she was than he had realized. He caught a trace of the light scent she wore, and it oddly brought to mind the vision of a high mountain meadow turned a solid blue by the lupine of late spring. Then he was looking across at a man propped against the pillows of a high-back mahogany bed.

Illness had left its faint shadow upon the face of Matthew Ladd. But his flannel nightgown couldn't hide the lines of a powerful, wide frame. The man's face was craggy, showing age but its muscles still firm. And the hazel eyes, exactly like his daughter's, now lighted with a pleasurable anticipation of this relief from boredom as he held out his hand.

"Wisdom. A sound handle. It's good meeting the man that pole-axed that brute, son."

His fist had an iron strength in it, and Wisdom was surprised by that into saying, "You're no sick man, sir."

" 'Course I'm not! Tell her what a mess o' nonsense Leatherwood's pumped into her." Ladd's glance shuttled to the girl. "Hear that, Sis? Today's my last in this confounded bed!"

"You'll stay there as long as the doctor says you should," Ann told him. Her glance touched Wisdom, once again holding that familiar quality of reserve as she nodded to a chair by the head of the bed. "Sit there and listen to him rave while I'm getting some coffee."

She had no sooner turned out the door than Matt Ladd was grinning broadly, proudly. "Was a time when I'd have traded her for a boy. Now I wouldn't swap her for two sons. She rides a tight herd on me and I like it."

He shifted higher against the pillows then, saying querulously, "This medico's nothing but a pill man. Wouldn't know heart trouble if he had it himself. Says one good dose of excitement will kill me off if I'm not careful! And here I feel fine."

"You look it."

The rancher's glance narrowed craftily, and in a lower tone he said, "Soon as she's out of the way you can grab a cigar out of the bureau drawer. I'll need a drag on it. Leatherwood, the old fool, has cut me down to one a day. What's the sense of a man hangin' on if he can't enjoy tobacco?"

"It's one of the few real pleasures." Wisdom took the chair now.

The glance the rancher put on him then was openly interested, judging. And abruptly Ladd was saying, "Tell me about yourself, son. It interests me to know what backs the man that can take Ray Myrick."

Wisdom shrugged. "Nothing much to tell."

"Where you from?"

"New Mexico Territory. Run some cattle above Cimarron."

"Cimarron? Isn't that Bob Robbins' country?"

Wisdom nodded, warily wondering if he should say more.

He decided finally that it didn't matter. "The judge was my father's friend."

The old man's face lighted up. "Y' don't say! Know what? Bob Robbins had a lot to do with my naming this brand. He used to try and get me sore by callin' me a brush-jumper. When I was tryin' to decide on a brand I remembered that and decided to call it Brush." He nodded to a framed picture hanging on the far wall above two crossed sabers. "Take a look at that and see if you can spot the judge."

Stepping over there, Wisdom eyed the photograph which showed a group of nine Union cavalrymen ranked facing the camera. Along the bottom ran the legend, *B Troop After Chickamauga. All That Were Left, September 19, 1863.*

Wisdom turned. "The judge is in the center, you're to his left."

Ladd chuckled delightedly. "There was a good man. Pity he's gone."

The girl came into the room just then and put a tray on the table at her father's bedside. On the tray were cups, a pewter urn and two matching bowls. She glanced around at Wisdom on her way back to the door, the unsettling seriousness in her eyes belying the levity of her words as she told him, "I'll no sooner be out of here than he'll offer you a cigar and then want to smoke it. Don't let him."

She went on out, closing the door behind her, and with a gusty sigh Matt Ladd nodded to the marble-topped bureau. "The right hand top drawer," he said gloomily.

Wisdom found a box of cigars there and lit one. He came over to the bed and offered it. But the rancher only shook his head, saying severely, "You heard what she said." And he nodded to the coffee.

He watched Wisdom closely as the coffee was poured and he took his cup. "Not wishin' to pry, son, but what brings you here?"

"After work."

"No, I mean why're you in this country?"

Wisdom tried to make his answer sound casual. "A man gets an itchy foot. Wants to travel around."

"So he does. Ann told you there was no job?"

"She did."

Ladd was wondering then if Ann could be the real reason

for this stranger having come here. That thought promoted
another that laid a soberness on his face as he studied Wisdom, telling himself, *He might be the one that could do it.*
He instinctively liked Wisdom's looks; and he had noticed a
seriousness in Ann which told him this man had impressed
her deeply, though he didn't understand exactly how that had
come about.

It was typical of Matthew Ladd's nature to waste no time
in over-carefully weighing decisions. His life had been a series
of such quick judgments, and in the main they had been
solid. He arrived at one of those decisions now, considered it
briefly, and followed his impulse by bluntly saying:

"Wisdom, I've got work for you if you'll take it. But I warn
you it's a chore you probably won't like. Furthermore, not a
soul's to know about it."

Surprised, Wisdom said, "Let's hear what it is."

Ladd frowned now, finding it difficult to choose his words.
"I tell you you won't like it. It'll be prying into a man's affairs,
spyin' on him."

"What man?"

The rancher hesitated before gravely saying, "I'd want your
word that this'll never go beyond the room. Not ever."

Wisdom nodded. "You have it."

Relieved on that point, Ladd went on irritably, "Ann's got
herself a man. Going to marry him. I want to know more
about him." At Wisdom's look of amazement, he added
hurriedly, "A fine thing for a father to be doin', eh? But this
happens to a father only once. I want it to be right for Ann."

Over a brief silence, Wisdom asked, "The man wouldn't
be Durwent, would he?"

"He would." The other's glance sharpened. "You know
him?"

"Met him this morning. Noticed your daughter with him."

Matt Ladd's face settled into a scowl. "Wouldn't be fair
to ask what you thought of him, so here's what I think.
George is a real gentleman. Folks have a hard time takin' to
him for that reason. I've made myself like him because of
Ann. But ..."

Waiting a long moment, Wisdom finally asked, "But
what?"

"Wish I knew." Ladd sighed heavily. "But let me tell you
of something that happened a couple weeks ago. We'd had a

rep down south on roundup over the county line. He brought me a story he'd got from a gent down there. This man had asked him if Jesse Ober and that Englishman up our way had any more giveaway buys on two year olds. Y' probably don't know Ober, but he's the nearest thing to a real hard case we have around here. This man went on to say he'd bought a batch of steers last spring from Ober on Durwent's bill of sale. When my man acted surprised and started askin' questions, this bird shut up and wouldn't say much more."

He paused, giving Wisdom a long look before he asked, "Now what do you make of that?"

"Could be someone hates Durwent bad enough to want to see him in trouble," Wisdom answered neutrally.

"Just what I thought at first," the rancher agreed. "On the other hand, this joker who did the talkin' is just the shady kind to cover up for anyone who'd sell him beef under the market, askin' no questions on where they came from. Of course, he'd never've said anything at all if he'd bought cattle at next to nothing. But what I ask myself is how Ober could've delivered steers backed by Durwent's bill of sale. Did Durwent only hire him for the delivery or were the two in on something off color?"

Wisdom only shrugged, and Ladd went on impatiently, "What's more to the point, George runs a two-bit layout. I know for a fact he's had at least two poor winters with hardly any beef at all to market."

There was nothing to say to that, so Wisdom waited. And then Matt Ladd was saying tiredly, "I don't know what to make of it. Damned if I do! Either something's in back of it, something I don't like one bit, or as you say this man was only trying to stir up trouble for George. Anyway, I've got to get the straight of it and it's something I can't ask George about."

"How would you set about getting the straight of it?"

"Hire you to hang around up there near George's place watchin' who comes and goes, to begin with." Ladd's glance turned quizzical. "Or maybe you could think of a better way of goin' about it."

Wisdom's instinct was to tell the man he didn't want to go at it any way at all. He was in this country for a far different reason than helping a father spy on a man because of his doubts about the soundness of a daughter's marriage. But then Wisdom all at once realized that here might be his chance of staying around Longbow without one major complication.

He spoke of that now, asking the rancher, "Suppose your law gets to wonderin' about me? What do I tell him? Or suppose Durwent spots me, gets suspicious and goes to your sheriff?"

"That's easy. John Cromer's spent half his life workin' for me. He's one of the best friends I've got. I'll slip him the word you're working for me and he won't mind what anybody says."

Wisdom's sober expression betrayed none of the satisfaction he took from this answer. "Anything else?" he asked. "About the only thing I know besides what you've told me is that Durwent came to me this morning with a proposition. Seems he wanted to match me with Myrick to clean up some easy money."

Matt Ladd swore soundly, profanely. "The fool! He'll gamble when he can't pay his grub bills! Though most times I'll admit he's lucky. He's even gambling on his marriage. I've offered to give him and Ann a ten section chunk of fine grass south of here, land they can borrow on to fix up his place. But he's got it in his head he'd rather have a hill strip off east closer to his place. Nothin' on it but timber and a coal pit. He says he wants to cut the timber, set up a sawmill and go into the lumber business. And here there's already a lumber yard in town."

"Maybe he figures he can sell the coal too."

"How could he sell coal?" Ladd growled. "Here we've got it on the place and never use it except for blacksmithin'. It's foul stuff, dirties up everything with smoke and soot. I lost a good cook once on account of buyin' him a coal range, tryin' to make him use it. I've told our neighbors if they want any of the stuff to come haul it away, much as they want. But I've still got to see the first load hauled."

As the older man ran out of words, Wisdom asked, "Anything else I ought to know about Durwent?"

Ladd thought a moment. "Nothin' else except about Ira. George works only one man, a damn' fine black man if ever there was one. I've tried to pump Ira, but he won't pump."

"Pump him how?"

"About who George's friends are, where he spends his time.

Ira's too confounded loyal to say a word. If you do prowl around up there, your game's up if Ira spots you. I wouldn't want him after me."

The rancher went silent then, and Wisdom knew the man was waiting for his answer. In this moment Wisdom was thinking of the girl, knowing she would despise him if he took her father's offer and she should ever discover what he was doing. And Ann Ladd's opinion of him did matter.

But then he saw that something far more than the girl's respect for him was involved here. Matt Ladd was opening the country to him, offering him safety from the law in his hunt for Ober.

So, with a deliberate shrug, he drawled, "Maybe I could help you."

Patience was as strong in Jesse Ober's makeup as was the thick-skinned tolerance with which he overlooked the distrustful attitude most people in this country showed him. As the day progressed, he used a full measure of that patience, and a great deal of caution, in observing Rush Wisdom's actions.

He knew, for instance, that Wisdom attended the inquest, that afterward he went to the hotel and didn't reappear again until almost one o'clock, at which time he ate a meal in Walt Heffran's restaurant. For two more hours Ober furtively observed the man either loafing on the street or in the stores, making a few purchases. Then, toward four o'clock, Wisdom hired a roan horse from Ned Arnholt, rode down to the hotel where he picked up a blanket roll, and left town along the upper valley road.

From then on a different quality of Ober's came into play. He was by natural bent a born hunter of both animal and human quarry, and when he left Longbow he cut across the hills straight for the foot of Spruce Ridge, as certain that Wisdom must be headed for this spot as he was certain that the lifting clouds would burn off before evening.

But, once on the river, he could find no cover that suited his purpose; for his judgment was that Wisdom could be dangerous, that he would have to be absolutely certain in what he'd set about doing. So he changed his plans, crossed the river, climbed the ridge and waited in the timber there.

He had been out of the saddle barely five minutes when

Ann Ladd came up the trail and stopped her bay horse nearby, for some minutes looking back down toward the river. Her lingering irritated him, for Wisdom should be coming along any minute. No sooner had the girl ridden on than he rode to the trail's edge and looked downward.

He was barely in time to see Wisdom cutting into some oak brush two hundred yards above the stream, headed this way. A strong excitement hit him then as he rode on back to tie the claybank gelding deeper in the trees and drew the Spencer rifle from its scabbard. He then walked back and picked himself cover, with a wide, unbroken field stretching toward the trail that was barely fifty yards distant. He judged it might be three or four more minutes before Wisdom passed this point, and again he used patience in denying himself a smoke during the interval.

At least five minutes passed, then two more. Worry began to thin Ober's high anticipation. It was all of another minute before he caught a distant hoof-rattle and looked around in time to see Wisdom sloping down off a higher hogsback a quarter mile back from the line of this ridge.

Ober breathed a deep, exasperated sigh, went back to the claybank and started a circle that would put him ahead of Wisdom once more.

But that beginning disappointment was only one of several as the afternoon faded into evening. Ober wasn't quite fast enough reaching a clump of jackpine two miles above Spruce Ridge. Arrived there, he saw Wisdom already several hundred yards further on along the road. And when he had made his second circle to a point well above Matt Ladd's place, all the reward he had for his pains was to watch Wisdom ride in on Brush.

He had a choice to make then, provided Wisdom left the ranch before the day was out. Making the choice, he decided the man would return to town. So he again circled and this time took a chance he didn't like in leaving the claybank in a shallow draw half a mile below Brush, then bellying down with the Spencer on a ledge near the crest of a high granite outcropping almost a hundred yards from the road. Half an hour went by, another twenty minutes. Then when Wisdom abruptly appeared, coming out Brush's lane some minutes after the sun had rimmed the far horizon, and when he turned on up the road instead of down, Ober cursed obscenely at this continuing run of poor luck.

But Jesse Ober was a man not to be denied what he had set his mind to, and he punished the claybank severely in swinging south at a high lope across an open stretch, then sharply east paralleling the road. He was a good man in the saddle, wiry, slight, and the gelding was sound, a stayer. When he had gone what he judged to be nearly two miles at that hard run, he swung back north.

He was aiming for a shallow notch where the road ran between timbered slopes, and he had gone too far, too close to the road, before he quite realized it. To reach the trees along the nearest side of the draw he once again had to cross open ground. He rode that stretch warily, fast, realizing he could be seen from the road. A minute's pause once he was in the trees showed him nothing moving along the road, and as he climbed the claybank through the timber he was sure he hadn't been seen and was well ahead of his quarry.

Some three minutes later he sighted the road once more, this time lying close below. He ground-haltered the claybank, drew the Spencer again and started at a slow run across the brushy slope. Noticing the poor light, his long face took on a worried scowl.

He was looking toward the road as he ran, and all at once saw what he wanted, a clear aisle down through the trees. He hauled up short, shallowing his breathing, listening. At first he could hear nothing. Then sharply across the stillness came a light, quick-cadenced flutter of hooves that snapped his nerves tight. He instantly recognized the sound as that of a deer taking flight, and quickly forgot it, intent upon placing himself so as best to see the road.

He was thinking now that he needn't have hurried, that there was plenty of time. He deliberately chose a grassy patch on which to lie, afterward stirring an elbow to move away a small stone, all the while listening intently for the sound of Wisdom's approach below. He had picked a wide, open lane through the trees as the spot along which his bullet was to travel. This was to be ridiculously easy. The road was in plain sight, not so much as a branch in the way. He held the Spencer cradled easily in both hands, ready.

All at once that easy confidence left him and he was wondering what had panicked the deer. The sound had come from his left along the slope. He quickly looked that way through the brushy undergrowth, but could see nothing. Then a hint of movement further to his left, at the very limit of his vision, made him move his shoulders around so as to see better.

There, thirty feet behind him, was Rush Wisdom's hunched over shape moving stealthily through the brush toward him.

Three

FOR POSSIBLY three seconds Jesse Ober lay there motionless, held rigid by the shock of disbelief and stark terror over the man he was stalking having stalked him. Wisdom came on another step. And a sudden uncontrollable panic drove Ober to throwing his body sideways in a violent roll. The Spencer was forgotten, all his instinct for preservation instantly centering on the handgun at his thigh.

His clawed fingers struck holster an audible blow that made Wisdom wheel more squarely this way. Too late, Ober realized that until this moment Wisdom hadn't seen him, that stealth would have meant a sure kill.

But now he saw Wisdom's hand arc a Colt's upward, very fast. His own lifted clear of leather viciously, with a choppy motion. He lined his weapon in a frantic haste to beat the explosion of that other weapon. Wisdom's .44 lanced sudden flame, and flying dirt stung the side of Ober's face at the moment the Colt's bucked hard against his wrist.

Never before had death beckoned to Ober so strongly. When he saw Wisdom's high shape drop abruptly behind the screening thicket, all he could think was that another bullet was on its way to him.

He thrashed his tough body around, scrambled to his feet and dove in behind the thick bole of the nearest pine eight feet away. Lunging erect again, he ran as hard as he could, keeping the tree between him and Wisdom. For ten reaching strides he expected each instant to feel the bone-smashing slam of a bullet into his spine.

Dodging frantically, not wanting to look behind him, not daring to, he picked the thickest cover. He put tree after tree, and one thicket after another, between him and the spot where he had last glimpsed Wisdom. His chest began heaving, exhaustion was crowding him, and still he ran his hardest in wild flight.

Coming suddenly on the claybank, he threw himself belly down across the saddle, forgetting reins and stirrups. With a vast, convulsive effort that left him trembling he managed to get a leg over the cantle as the animal plunged away in fright. The horse was headed straight back in Wisdom's direction, and he bent down, managing finally to snatch the leathers and saw the animal into a tight turn. He stayed hunched over as he reined recklessly off through the trees. It wasn't until he had covered all of two hundred yards that an abrupt relief flowed through him, and he knew he was safe for the moment, out of range.

Only when he straightened in the saddle did he remember the Spencer he'd left lying back there. Then he became aware that he was still clenching the Colt's in a grip that made his knuckles ache. The panic in him started thinning then, and he put curse after curse upon Wisdom, hating the man for having tricked him, for having shown him depths of fear he had never before known.

Most of this day had made it a kind John Cromer hated above all others, a day indoors. Since the inquest, he hadn't been outside the building once except for a quick trip down the street to Walt Heffran's for the noon meal.

As the afternoon wore on he had doggedly disposed of the accumulated paper work on his desk, wishing he could be out in the weather, bad as it was. His ledger had to be readied for the coming meeting of the county commissioners. He had to write two long overdue letters. Finally, well past four o'clock, he had taken a pad of telegraph forms from a drawer of his desk and stared for some minutes at it, facing a chore he had been putting off since early morning.

His thoughts then revolved about the matter he had almost, but not quite, mentioned to Ann Ladd this morning. At length, he commenced writing in his precise but labored way: *Warden, Territorial Prison, Yuma, Terr. Arizona. Please notify* . . .

The look of this beginning displeased him. Scowling down at it, he left the address, crossed out the two words of the message and began over again: *Advise at once whereabouts of prisoner named Lockhart sent you from Laramie last* . . .

Leaning back in his chair, he tried to remember the month of the Laramie trial. Abruptly then, with a mutter of disgust, he tore the sheet from the pad, crumpled it and walked across to throw it in the fire. Back at the desk again, he sighed in wonder over ever having let Matt Ladd talk him into leaving Brush for this unwanted job of regulating other men's affairs.

Still, his conscience called on him to act officially on his suspicions, and he slowly penned another message, addressing it as he had the first:

> Estate of relative to Lockhart prisoner sent you
> last spring from Laramie being probated here.
> Advise this office name of Yuma attorney to
> handle legal negotiations.
>
> Cromer, Sheriff.

The awkward wording of the telegram and the fact of having given away nothing in it pleased Cromer. In his deliberate way he had stumbled upon a means of getting information while giving none. Satisfied, he put on coat and hat and started on down the street to the post office at Kramer's store, the light drizzle and the cold a welcome relief from his stuffy office.

He was on his way across the intersection below the courthouse when he saw Ray Myrick standing on the corner dead ahead. He didn't particularly want any words with the man, so he thrust hands deep in pockets and scowled down at the walk when he reached it, looking neither left nor right. He had already passed the man when Myrick's deep voice sounded querulously:—

"Not speakin' to your friends today, John?"

Cromer looked around, pretending surprise, saying with a false heartiness. "Why sure, Ray. How goes it?"

"Not good." Myrick's rueful grin showed how stiff the right side of his face was with its gash at the corner of the mouth and that whole cheek so swollen the eye was barely slitted open.

Though he'd had the details of the fight, it was still a shock to the law man to see how badly the big man's face was battered. "You don't look good," he said. "Well, anything can happen."

Myrick's glance turned quickly belligerent. "He couldn't do it again in a hundred tries. Couldn't touch me."

"That so?"

"That's so." At Cromer's neutral nod, Myrick added, "And I aim to prove it."

"Your privilege."

"Just thought you ought to know, sheriff."

There was a challenge in the way the big man made his statement. It didn't escape Cromer. He knew Myrick had never particularly liked him. Nevertheless, he tried to keep his personal feeling out of it as he said, "Just stick to your fists and it'll be okay with me, Ray." He went on then, not wanting to give the other a chance to make an argument of it.

He gave the clerk at Kramer's store two dollars, with instructions that the telegram was to be dropped off at the station in Junction by the driver of tonight's stage. Then, on his way out of Kramer's, he saw Martha Burke on her way into Elder's Market across the street.

Sight of the girl at once took his mind off Frank Lockhart's nearly-forgotten letter and the probability of this newcomer, Rush Wisdom, being any relation to that other Wisdom, let alone his killer. He stood there under the store awning considering something far more pleasant, though quite alien to his state of strict bachelorhood.

Ordinarily there was little subtlety in John Cromer. But it was that glimpse of Martha Burke that shortly sent him on down the street and then across the mud to Ennis's pool parlor. His happening to come out onto the walk some ten minutes later, just as Martha was approaching, gave every appearance of their meeting being accidental.

Martha was laden with two well filled baskets and holding an umbrella. She gladly accepted his offer of carrying the baskets on home for her. Once there, she insisted he stay for what she called afternoon tea. It turned out to be not tea at all but some of the best coffee he'd tasted in weeks, along with crumb cake dusted with cinnamoned sugar she mixed and baked as he watched.

This somehow intimate moment, their being together in the kitchen, prompted Cromer at one point to say miserably, "Mart, this gets worse the longer it goes on."

"What does?" Kneeling before the oven, she glanced around at him.

Her guilelessness, and the trusting, affectionate look she put upon him, brought him across to her then to take her by the elbows, lift her and put his arms around her. When he felt her stiffen, he had said, "Stop that!" Then, putting a finger under her chin, he tilted her face up and kissed her.

He could sense the effect of their long embrace, the gradual relaxing and the giving in her. Then, quite as suddenly as the notion had struck him, he was regretting what he had done. Taking her by the arms, he pushed her gently away, looking down at her to ask gravely, "Doesn't this mean anything to you, Mart?"

"Of course it does." Shyness came over her then and she turned from him, saying hurriedly, "You're going to be eating burnt cake if you don't let the cook alone, John." She knelt, opened the oven door to test the cake with a broom straw, then took the pan out and carried it over to the zinc drainboard alongside the cistern pump.

Cromer, watching her, longing for her, took out his pipe and packed it. Lighting it, he had stated deliberately, "We will be married before Christmas, before your birthday," speaking as forcefully as he knew how, not listening to an inner voice that mocked his words.

"Please don't remind me of another birthday, John," was Martha's way of ignoring the real point of his statement. Her back was to him as she cut the cake and put it on a plate, asking, "Doesn't a woman become an old maid when she turns thirty?"

"No more than a man with my inclination does when he's thirty-eight. Even if his hair is white." He knew he had a point to make here, something they had never before spoken of. And he went on stubbornly, "Your father will come to live with us. Or, better yet, we'll rent this house from him so he won't have to move the shop. We can put on another room or two in back here. This can be another bedroom, with the kitchen on behind."

She turned slowly to face him, her paleness and a look akin to terror in her blue eyes utterly bewildering him. "John, I won't have this!" she said, low-voiced. "You're hurting me! Pop has always insisted he'll live alone if I ever marry. You know he can't! And you—"

"Dear God! You're a woman, aren't you? You need a man, a husband! And kids, a whole houseful of kids! Fred Burke's as able as I am to live by himself. He's got a responsibility as a father to let you . . . to make you . . ."

Helplessly checking his outburst, he ran a hand across his eyes as he sighed. "I'm sorry, Mart. Sorry as can be."

"One thing you must understand, John," she said in a

voice barely audible. "Pop has time and again told me exactly what you just have. He's not as selfish as you suppose. But—"

"Did I ever call him selfish?"

"No, not in so many words. But you must think he is. The truth of it is that he's a child in one way. Worse than a child. You know as much about that as I. Here I've been away in Junction for only two days and come home to find him in trouble. You must know I can't leave him."

She saw him about to interrupt, lifted a hand to silence him; and her eyes were brimming with tears. "I won't burden you or any other man with him. I ..." Her glance dropped away in embarrassment. "Now let's not talk about it any longer."

Later, the cake plate empty and their cups nearly so, Cromer broke a long silence by all at once asking, "What can you tell me about Wisdom, Mart?"

She gave him a puzzled look. "What is there to tell? You know as much about him as I. Except for what he did last night. It was ... well, something Barney and Ed Bone had been afraid to try."

His interest quickened. "What was that?"

"Carried me out of that wash. Barney was all for our staying with the stage. And Bone insisted it was safest, said the water wouldn't get high enough to harm us. They had left us there, taken the horses across. Wisdom and I were alone. Then all at once he took matters into his own hands."

"How?" Cromer asked worriedly. "You said nothing about this!"

"No. Because I haven't seen you till now, John. What he did was decide we weren't safe in the stage. I insisted we were. He wouldn't listen, and got out. I wanted to stay there. He was perfectly gentlemanly about it, but finally he stopped arguing and pulled me out."

"Pulled you? Roughed you?" Cromer asked indignantly.

"I suppose he did rough me. I ... well, I fought him for a minute. Until he took me in his arms and started wading. Then all I could do was hold onto him and pray we wouldn't drown. I was terrible afraid."

Angrily, Cromer breathed, "I'll speak to the man about that!"

"But you won't, John. You see, he was right. We'd barely made the bank when Bone called to us to look back. There was the stage going over, breaking up. If Wisdom had let me stay there, I wouldn't be here now."

The sheriff breathed a long, worried sigh, scowling down at the table to say finally, "The man has put me in his debt. I wish he hadn't."

"Why, John?"

"Because," Cromer solemnly replied, "I may have no way but one of repaying him. And it's a way not to my credit."

"What in heaven's name are you talking about?"

"That is something I trust you will never know, Martha, never."

This was George Durwent's third attempt at writing the letter, and he found it as unsatisfactory as the other two had been. He crumpled the sheet, held it over the lamp's chimney till it caught fire, then slouched low in the chair, scowling at it as it burned.

All but one corner of it had curled to grey ash when he heard Ira's step coming along the hallway from the kitchen. He dropped the page into the table's ash tray and was scrubbing it to powder with forefinger as Ira came into the room.

"Someone out there, Mist' George."

Durwent looked around, his expression convincingly bored. "Out where?"

"In back." The black man was towelling a kettle that had held their supper's stew. His head tilted toward the rear of the house. "It's either somebody horseback or a skunk prowlin' up by the cold cellar. Want I should go take a look?"

"I'll go."

Durwent was rising from his chair as Ira said, "We could sure use a dog around here, boss."

"And have him howling all night at every shadow and sound?" Durwent asked dryly on his way out the door.

He went on around the house quickly, impatient with himself for not having been more alert, for having given Ira this one more minor detail to add to what he already knew or had guessed. His insistence on not having a dog around the place, for instance, was a contradiction to what Ira knew of him, for in the old days he'd never been without a hunting dog constantly at his heels. He sometimes wondered what Ira made of these inconsistencies, like his going out now and pretending to look around when Ira knew him to be too lazy ordinarily to think of doing such a thing.

It was dark enough so that the weak indigo was fading along the western horizon, and he chose his direction from the black, squat out-line of the root cellar at the upper end of the house clearing. He was thirty feet from it when he made out the shape of a horse and rider standing there. Then shortly Jesse Ober's voice was sounding across to him in a hushed, querulous tone:—

"What took you so long? You said seven. It's after."

"Didn't hear you," Durwent answered as he came up to the man. Then at once he asked, "Any luck?"

"None at all," came Ober's dry answer. He looked down at the house then, toward the light in the kitchen window. "Ira know I'm here?"

"Forget Ira. What news of our friend?"

Ober ignored the question, drawling, "You trust that black son a lot beyond what I would."

"Forget him, I said." ... Durwent's voice was edged with irritation and a faint scorn ... "I'd cut his black heart out if he ever went against me by so much as one word. He knows that. He's bound to me, a slave."

"Thought there wasn't no slaves no more."

Durwent sighed audibly in disgust. "Jesse, I'm a British subject. Ira was bought in Barbados. Whether you like it or not, he's a slave. Now what about Wisdom?"

Briefly, yet leaving nothing important unsaid, Ober dryly recounted his poor fortunes of the afternoon and evening, ending by saying, "For a fact, he outguessed me. I'm in luck to be here."

"You let him outdraw you?" Durwent was incredulous.

"Outdraw, hell! I was layin' on my back."

Durwent's awe held him silent a long moment. Then: "Was he close enough to recognize you?"

"He was close enough to count the buttons on my shirt," came Ober's dour reply.

"You say he shot only once, then went down?"

"That's right."

"Couldn't that mean you got him?"

"Could. Or it couldn't."

"You'll have to go back there and make sure, Jesse."

"Not me!"

This was a new Jesse Ober, a strange one. Durwent could scarcely believe what he was hearing. But over his surprise he now asked guilefully, "Afraid of him, Jesse?"

"Damn' right I am!"

"If he's still alive, he'll be after you. Tomorrow. Or the next day, or the next."

"Let him come. I got help up at the place."

Durwent checked his anger at the other's rebellion, saying, "What kind of help do you call it? Is there a man with you who wouldn't sell you out?" He paused, letting the words sink in. "He may find a way of getting to you, Jesse."

Ober shrugged. "I could always pull out. What's to keep me from driftin'? I got nothin' here a hundred dollars couldn't buy twice."

"You'd throw all this over because of a run of poor luck?" Durwent laughed softly, with mockery in his tone. "All you've gambled so far? All that's to come?"

He sensed Ober's narrow glance on him even before Ober softly drawled, "Any time you feel like tellin' me what this is all about, I'll manage to listen."

"You know what it's all about."

"Sure. This now. But in Laramie you only told me what to do, never why it was bein' done."

Durwent was several seconds finding an answer to that, at length saying, "It's because of Wisdom's name, Jesse. His name."

"His name? What about it? And which name, Wisdom or Lockhart? Today's the first time I ever run onto that handle Wisdom."

"Get rid of him and you'll probably never hear it again."

Ober made no sense whatsoever of Durwent's words. It was often this way with certain things Durwent told him. Sometimes, usually a long time afterward, he'd connect an unlooked-for happening to a comment of the Englishman's. But more often than not he would never understand the riddle of the man's most enigmatic remarks. Though it had so far paid him not to be too curious, what had happened tonight gave him the right to demand something more definite of Durwent.

So now he asked, "Does this gent have to wind up where friend Idaho did?"

"That's up to you, Jesse."

"Why only to me? To you too, ain't it?" Ober saw the

other's head tilt up sharply in anger, went on, "You been dealin' me short so far, George. You talk about what's comin' without ever sayin' what it is. Now's the time for some straight talk."

"Then here is some," came Durwent's unhesitating words. "Go back there tonight, make sure of Wisdom and you'll get another bill of sale for more steers. For thirty this time."

Ober shook his head. "I said we need straight talk. Like what you're doin', why you want this Wisdom under the sod."

"For thirty head you wouldn't have to know, would you, Jesse? That would mean at least four hundred dollars in your pocket."

Ober sat considering this, a measure of his patience returning. It was obvious that Durwent wasn't going to share any confidence. It was just as obvious that the man put great store in having Wisdom out of the way.

Jesse Ober had never been a poor hand at driving a bargain, and now he said, "You got to pay for this kind of chore. Y'know that, don't you?"

"I am paying. Four hundred."

"Hunh-uh." Ober moved his head deliberately from side to side. "You're payin' more, Durwent. A lot more. Either I help myself to fifty head or I pull out. This country's gettin' a mite warm for me anyway."

"Fifty!" Durwent exploded, nevertheless keeping his voice low. "That'll nearly wipe me out! I could maybe make it thirty-five, but—"

"But fifty's what I ask," Ober cut in. "And don't worry about bein' cleaned out. I'll spread it over a couple months. You can give me say three bills of sale. I'll help myself to the biggest bunch come the first good snow. Your winter kill's always high. Blame it on that if anyone asks why your herd's gone so thin."

George Durwent had never relied greatly on profanity, but rather on polished invective of a distinctly original turn. Now, however, he cursed like the commonest cowhand, afterward protesting, "Fifty and I'm ruined, out of business!"

"But you got this other comin' along, whatever it is," Ober reminded him. "And you got the girl. Married to her, your worries are over."

"I'll go as high as thirty-seven, Jesse. Take that or nothing."

"Nothin' it is, then." Ober pulled the claybank's head around, obviously on the point of leaving.

With a long sigh, Durwent said quickly, "All right, this time you have it your way. But I don't want any bills of sale shown in this country again. Rework your brands and take them east, at least a hundred miles."

"Easy enough."

"Another thing. I want Wisdom to disappear completely. Understand? No one here knows him, so no one will think twice if he drops out of sight."

Ober nodded. "One of those rotten ledges up Horse Lake way ought to take care of that."

"You don't have any notion why he went to see Ladd?"

"Not any."

"I can find out tomorrow," Durwent said musingly. Then: "Better meet me in town first thing in the morning so I'll know how you came out. Be careful, Jesse. This thing can pay off in a big way. For both of us."

"Can it?" Ober waited for an answer. When none came, he held out a hand, his left.

Durwent caught the meaning of the gesture, asking dryly, "Won't tomorrow do?"

"Now would be better, George."

Durwent turned without another word and went back down to the house. He entered the main room as quietly as he could, took paper, ink and a pen from the table, came out onto the porch again. There, by the lamplight shining through the window, he wrote out three bills of sale, the first for twenty-two steers, the second for seventeen; he hesitated over the third, finally making it for ten.

He walked slowly on up to the root cellar the second time, saying as he handed the papers to Ober, "Those work only when you've finished the job, Jesse. If it takes you a week or a month."

Ober said, "Okay." Then he did a thing Durwent had feared he might. Taking out a match, he flicked it alight with thumbnail and stared down at the bills of sale.

With Durwent's face clear in the match's flare, Ober shortly gave him a deliberate glance, drawling. "Your arithmetic's poor, friend. These add only to forty-nine."

Durwent's look took on definite haughtiness. "Add them again."

Ober smiled thinly, coldly, folding the sheets and thrusting them in shirt pocket as he dropped the match. "No matter. You'll make it up to me one way or another."

So saying, he reined around and away, leaving Durwent speechless with a rising, sultry anger. Durwent glared at the man's shape fading into the obscurity of the nearby timber, afterward catching in the dying out of the claybank's hoof falls against the night's humming stillness a quality of whispering, mocking laughter.

George Durwent had always looked upon Ober as being far beneath him, a man of lesser intelligence whose singular capabilities were to be bought without his personality entering into their relations. Now, realizing that this mere hireling had caught him in a niggardly act, he saw that Ober had assumed a real identity for the first time in all their dealings. He found himself hating the man venomously, with an intensity that made him almost wish it could be Wisdom, not Ober, who was to come through this night alive.

That startling thought had no sooner taken form than he was considering it as a real possibility. And, because of it, he knew he must get the letter written to Alfred tonight and have Ira take it in to catch tomorrow's early stage, whether or not it pleased him to put certain things on paper.

That first instant of consciousness, Wisdom was aware only of a thorny prickling against his face and shoulders. The next came a hammer blow of pain that threatened to split open the side of his head. He groaned in agony at the second pulse pound, not understanding where he was, or why. But then he felt the rough horn handle of the Colt's against his palm and remembered.

He found the strength to roll onto his back, open his eyes. The effort left him breathing hard, and the pain in his head took on a blinding intensity. There was a damp coolness above his right temple, and he lifted a hand, gingerly running forefinger along a raw tear in the scalp there. The starlight was strong enough to let him see a dark streak across his hand when he took it away. And now that last split-second of consciousness came back to him and he was seeing his bullet pick up black earth perhaps four inches to one side of Jesse Ober's fear-frozen face. At that instant a crushing blow had struck him at the side of the head to blot out all his awareness.

Slowly, over the pain, he considered the enigma of Ober not having finished what he had set out to do. Some of the stoicism Yuma had put in him let him ignore the throbbing in his brain then and rationally look upward through the crest of a nearby pine to study the night sky's cloudpatched dusting of stars. At the end of a considerable interval he decided he must have been lying here upward of an hour's time.

He began to think about moving, and wondered how long it would take him to get back down the slope and along the road to where he had tied the roan. That fleeting glimpse he'd had of Ober running the claybank across the open stretch short of the draw had saved his life, though the bolting of the muletail through the brush some minutes afterward had considerably narrowed the margin of his advantage over the man. Pure chance had let Ober sight him first. And pure chance again had thrown the man's bullet wide by that fraction of an inch that meant the difference between a kill and a near one.

Presently, he rolled over again and face down in the thorny tangle of the wild rose thicket, and then laboriously got to his knees. The sting of the thorns was something to be thankful for, since it made him less conscious of the torture in his brain. Only when he could sit back against his heels did he weakly shove the Colt's into holster and begin resting for the greater effort of standing. The night's deep shadows were wheeling crazily before his vision and nausea was plaguing him. He tried not to let his thoughts dwell on the failure of his one shot, telling himself that this disappointment needn't matter. He would have another chance at Frank's killer. He wouldn't fail the second time.

He was sitting there with chin on chest, hoping for an easing off of the maul-pound in his head, when a whisper of sound penetrated his dulled awareness. He lifted his head, straining to listen. Shortly the sound came again, more distinctly. He finally defined it as the low crunch of gravel under some weighty object. And suddenly all his senses were keened to danger, the pain in his head forgotten as he eased the Colt's from its scabbard again.

He waited motionless, breathing shallowly for perhaps three minutes. Then abruptly through the branches of the bush he caught a hint of movement close by a mass of black shadowed undergrowth some twenty yards to his left. He lost whatever it was the next moment, for it moved in line with the brush.

There was a brief interval when his wariness relaxed on remembering the muletail, and he was thinking that this could be another deer.

With sudden startlement, he saw a moving shape detach itself from the darker background and start obliquely toward him. It took him but a moment to define that blocky shadow as a man's stooped form.

Carefully, soundlessly, he drew back the hammer of the .44, pressing trigger to avoid the click of the sear. Over this brief space of time he watched the man close on him, soundlessly stalking.

He was lifting his weapon into line when, from far down along the road, the distant and muted thud of a trotting horse's hooves whispered restlessly in across the stillness. He saw the man hesitate the moment the sound came, saw him turn slowly about and start away.

Straightening on his knees, Wisdom called, "Ober!"

He saw the shape lunge erect and hard to one side. A lightning crack of gun-thunder, along with a rosy stab of flame, exploded at him across the still night. And now the man's thin shape was unmistakably Ober's.

Wisdom surged unsteadily to his feet, wanting nothing to spoil his target. He aimed carefully against his dizziness as the man wheeled violently once more. And the blast of his .44 prolonged the second echo of that other weapon.

He saw his first bullet slam Ober backward in a broken stagger. He saw his second, thrown in savage fury, knock the man off balance. His third drove that falling shape on around in a drunken lurch that turned Ober all the way onto his back as he slumped to the ground.

Wisdom lowered the Colt's, checking the impulse to fire again. He took one step toward that prone, loose figure, and the brush tripped him and he fell full length. Once again he was feeling the sharp gouging of the thorns against face and arms, and for long seconds the blasting of pain in his head deafened him, drained him of all strength.

As the pain and the ringing in his ears slowly slacked away, a cadenced hoof rattle rolled up through the timber from the direction of the road. He paid the sound as little attention as he did the punishment he gave his hands pushing against the tangle of roots and branches, trying to come to his knees again.

A voice from close below called sharply, "Who's there?

Wisdom?" and he looked out through the branches and saw a horse run out of the shadows, and the rider pull in hard alongside Ober's sprawled shape.

It was Ann Ladd, and she looked this way now at the sound of Wisdom heaving himself to his knees once more. She put her horse across here with an ungentle sawing of reins and strike of spur. Before the animal could answer the tightening of the leathers, she had swung aground close in to the thicket and was pushing through it, crying, "Wisdom! What's happened?"

He tried to speak. But a sudden weakness and dizziness in him brought nothing forth beyond a hoarse croaking. So he tried to shake his head as she knelt beside him and put an arm about his shoulders. The movement of his head turned him giddy, the pain laying a thickening grey curtain over all his senses.

The girl caught him as he slumped forward, unconscious.

Matt Ladd faintly heard the sound of a horse running down the upper road and with some alarm guessed that it meant trouble. He had some minutes ago left his bed to lift the window wider open and clear out the room's stale air. Now he got out of bed a second time, going straight to the high mahogany wardrobe for the clothes he hadn't worn in almost three weeks.

By the time he had dressed, he was more excited than worried; for this was a solid excuse for ending his long siege that had rarely taken him beyond the room's confines. He was looking forward to what was coming, whatever that might be.

Something like an hour ago he had tried to argue Ann out of her night ride, tried to tell her that the sound of the guns she had heard rolling down so faintly out of the eastward hills might mean anything. It could be some rider trying for a loafer or an owl. Or perhaps she had imagined that the sounds were shots, for he hadn't heard them.

But she had insisted that the shots came too close together to have been fired by only one gun. Since there were two, she argued, they could well mean trouble. And in her willful way she had gone regardless of her father's scoffing. He had supposed that her going was only an excuse for being alone, for working off that strange restlessness that had been in her since late afternoon.

He wasn't at all sure that Ann was the rider he was hearing now until the sound had gathered volume enough to tell him that whoever it was had turned up the house lane. He was waiting on the porch as she brought her badly winded mare across the yard and in to the rail at the foot of the steps.

Sight of him made her say, "Back to bed you go!" as she stepped out of the saddle. But on her way up the steps she forgot his truancy, bursting out, "It's Wisdom, dad! He's badly hurt. And Ober's dead. I need help."

"Wisdom?" Shock held him speechless as she came up alongside him. He noticed only then that her eyes were wide with fear, and he managed to get out, "You mean he's killed Jesse Ober?"

She nodded, saying helplessly, "I don't know how it happened. But I was right below them when they shot it out. What can we do? He may be dying! I'd found his horse, that roan of Arnholt's there by the road. Then I ... then came these shots from up in the timber and ... Dad, help me!"

He saw that she was on the verge of tears, and he took her by the arms, gripping them tightly. "Where's your nerve gone, Sis? Of course I'll help."

She pulled away, starting back down the steps. "I'll get Bryant and maybe someone else."

"Wait!" He spoke sharply, his thoughts already having turned to his conversation with Wisdom this afternoon, to its possible bearing on what had happened to the man tonight. And now he thought quickly, almost afraid of what the night held in prospect for him, shortly telling her, "You'll hitch the greys to the surrey and bring it here. If one of the boys offers to help, so much the better. But not a word of this to anyone. We can manage between the two of us."

She stared up at him in strong surprise, and the lamplight from the room behind let him see her paleness and her look of panic. "You mean—"

"I mean I'm going with you. Now mind, I know what I'm talking about! This isn't going to hurt me. Wisdom's in trouble and no one's to know."

"Trouble. Do you know what it is?"

"How could I?" he asked gruffly, jolted by her sure intuition. He knew his denial to be only a half-truth, but went on, "We'll give him the benefit of a doubt till we know more. Get out there and hitch the team. If anyone asks what all the fuss is about, tell him I've kicked over the traces and won't stay in bed. You're taking me out for some night air, for a ride over to see George."

"But what if they heard the shots?"

"You don't know anything about that. Now get a move on!"

His impatience had become as strong as hers by the time she drove the surrey up the lane some ten minutes later. He took the reins, and they had gone hardly two hundred yards before Ann said miserably, "You're not hurrying! Can't we go faster?"

"And have every man out of the bunkhouse taggin' along after us, wonderin' what's up? Don't lose your head, girl."

They were nearly twenty minutes on the road, and during that interval Ann got a tight enough hold on her emotions to discuss what had happened rationally.

"I can't begin to understand it," she said when they were still half a mile short of the timbered draw. "Two men fighting it out in the dark. How could they possibly have met each other?"

"We'll know that when we talk to Wisdom."

"But he can't talk. He fainted."

"Where was he hurt?"

"Along the side of the head. His scalp's torn, bleeding." ... She was making an effort to keep her voice steady, to keep it from breaking ... "I tore off the tail of his shirt to bind it."

"How's his heart?" Ladd's tone was utterly grave.

"It was steady, not too fast. He was breathing just like he was asleep."

"Nothing to worry about then." The rancher nevertheless slapped the greys across rumps with the leathers, putting them on at a stiffer trot.

Finally, after what seemed an interminable length of time to them both, the surrey's lamps showed them the roan standing off to the side of the left wheel-rut. Passing the animal, they saw its reins wound loosely in the branches of a scrub oak thicket on the bank above.

Ann said then, "I don't quite know why this has hit me so hard, dad. Sorry I made such a fool of myself."

"I took to him right off, too, Sis."

Ann's head came quickly around. "To Wisdom, you mean?"

"Who else?"

She was silent a long moment, and the ring of the rig's tires echoed back from the timber now close at hand. Abruptly she said, "Turn off to the right beyond that next tree, the big one. And you're wrong about my taking to Wisdom. He's just another . . . well, nobody, as far as I'm concerned."

"Sure," Matt Ladd agreed with a pointed solemnity. "Just nobody."

"I'm not the least bit taken by him, if that's what you're trying to say. He gets in a brawl the first minute he hits town. He . . . Now he's been in another, killed a man."

"He sure picked the right one to kill."

"He's hurt and hurt badly," Ann said ignoring the pointedness of the father's comment. "I'd do this much for just anyone. Wouldn't you?"

Ladd put the team around the tree and slapped reins impatiently as the animals slowed to the climb. "It's been a long time since I've heard you talk such nonsense," he said.

She had no answer to that as she leaned forward now, studying the shadows beyond the reach of the lamps. Shortly she said, "More to the right," and as they came to an opening through the trees she spoke again. "Straight up now."

In ten more seconds she was up off the seat, standing, holding to the splash board as she peered into the upward darkness. Then suddenly she cried, "Stop."

Matt Ladd drew rein, and after the rig's wheels had paused in their slow arc she looked down at him incredulously to say in a hushed voice, "They're gone! Both of them!"

Four

THE LENGTHENING night took on an endless quality for Ann Ladd. Incongruous as it was, in the wakeful intervals that so often interrupted her fitful sleep she could think of nothing but Wisdom and what might have happened to him.

It didn't matter that she had known this man only a day, that he was almost a stranger. The fact remained that some indefinable quality in his makeup had so strongly impressed her that she was now extremely worried about him. And time and again, seeing her concern as being absurd, she would force her mind to dwell on other things, things that had lately become so all important, so pleasing to contemplate.

First of all there was George Durwent. She cast back over her two year acquaintance with him, recalling the minutest details of their courtship. But tonight her emotions seemed headstrong, wanting to go their own way, and she couldn't rouse the usual warmth of her feelings toward him.

She thought back over the plans for rebuilding Durwent's frame house, much in need of repair. She even tried to settle once and for all on the disputed pattern of the dining and bedroom wallpapers. She even began wondering what luck George would have in turning from cattle to lumber and coal, putting down the faint amusement that always struck her when she tried to think of him as a merchant, having to be civil to any and all customers.

But this weighing of the future, so indeterminate and unforeseeable, was far overbalanced by her apprehension over the present. Finally understanding this, her thoughts came back to Wisdom with an intensity that couldn't be denied. Quite honestly then, she had to admit that in certain ways she was strongly attracted to him. There was a graciousness about the man, an unobtrusive gentleness in him that was in essence true courtesy. She was certain that he was considerate. And, strangely, she found herself wishing that these

67

traits could be made a part of George's make-up, replacing his stilted and sometimes aloof manner.

Once in her troubled sleep, Jesse Ober's thin face with its bullet hole under the right eye haunted her and Wisdom on a long ride they made together up a steep climbing hill they never quite managed to crest. Throughout the dream, she held tightly to Wisdom's hand; she could feel its strength, and at the same time its gentleness, each time it would pull her out of Ober's reach. Waking from that nightmare, she was suddenly no longer able to stand the uncertainty over what had happened to him.

She got out of bed and dressed in the dark, shivering against the night's chill that seemed to penetrate as deep mentally as it did physically. She carried her short wool coat and her boots across the main room, walking as quietly as she could. In the kitchen she paused long enough to drink two lukewarm cups of coffee from the pot the cook always kept by the flue in the warming oven. She left the house by way of the kitchen door.

Making a wide circle to the lower corral to avoid barnlot and bunkhouse, she found her old saddle where she had hoped it would be, in the lean-to close by. She caught up the first animal that would stand to the rope. It turned out to be one of her father's geldings, a big, white-stockinged black, and she was able to take him from the corral and start east across the meadow without even having roused the dog that always slept outside the bunkhouse door.

The black was impatient to go, yet she held him down to a walk for all of a mile, wanting to take no chance on anyone hearing her even at a distance. There was plenty of time for what she had set out to do. She was cutting straight across the hills to that draw where she had last seen Wisdom.

A glance into the blackness overhead only deepened her poor spirits. Solid cloud hid the stars now, and she thought dismally that more rain must be on the way. This prospect seemed to suit her mood, and as the minutes slowly passed, the chill keeping her tense, she was groping for even the slightest understanding of what could have happened to Wisdom.

What she and her father had been able to see in the poor light of the surrey's lamps there along the brushy slope had confounded them both. There had been several of Wisdom's boot prints, their pattern elongated in a way that showed he had staggered as he walked, barely able to keep to his feet. Where Ober's body had lain they found a darkly glistening stain on the grass, and the topsoil beyond dragged smooth. Nearby were the shoe marks of a horse, and more of Wisdom's boot prints It was as though some rider had miraculously appeared to take Wisdom behind him on the saddle and drag Ober's body away.

But hardest of all to believe was what she and her father discovered as they started home. They had decided to take the roan on back to Brush with them. Yet when they reached the spot where the animal had been standing, he was no longer there. During the time they had been up the slope, someone, Wisdom she hoped, had furtively ridden the animal away.

Deeper than the enigma of Wisdom's disappearance ran her wonder over Matt Ladd's strange attitude toward the night's happenings. His insistence that no one know of them confounded her as much as his refusal to explain that insistence. His answer to her suggestion that she ride straight in to Longbow to get John Cromer had been an explosive:—

"Damn it, must you make it worse for him? The man's in real trouble!"

"But we know he killed Ober," she had insisted, more to try and gauge the measure of Wisdom's offense than in any real conviction of his wrongdoing.

"From what you say, it was either Ober or him."

"It was, dad I'm sure of that."

"Then good riddance. Jesse was long overdue for a finish like this In Wisdom's place, I'd have done the same. So would you. So stop talking hogwash!"

"Still, he did kill, didn't he?"

"He did. Because he had to. Which sometimes happens to the good as well as the bad. If I'm any judge, he's one of the good ones."

This attitude in her father made it seem almost as though he was hiding something. some knowledge of Wisdom that was being denied her. Nevertheless, that attitude she found strangely paralleling her own. She believed in Wisdom intuitively, despite her conviction that he had known Black, or Idaho, as she now thought of the man He had even possibly recognized Ober there on the street yesterday morning. This possibility of his having known two such shady characters didn't at all fit the impression he had given her, and it laid a deep undercurrent of mystery beneath her attempts at understanding how he and Ober had come to face each other in a shoot out. Stranger still was the time and place of their meeting.

A faint tinge of grey paling the blackness of the cloud mantle over the peaks finally made her thrust all these imponderables from mind and put the black on at a faster pace. But she arrived along the slope marked by the surrey's tire tracks long before the curtained dawn light had strengthened enough to let her see the ground clearly. And as she waited there, her exhalations laying a misty vapor before her face, the abrupt realization that Wisdom might have died during the night tightened her already tense apprehension.

John Cromer had years ago taught her to read sign, imparting to her a good measure of his skill. Though she hadn't done much tracking for years, enough of the art had stayed with her to make that first hour of the day's wan light along the slope a profitable one At the end of it, the ground had told her several things

First, Wisdom had trudged back and forth across the side of the hill until he had come upon a horse tied deep in a chokeberry thicket This had been after she had left him and gone home for help The horse she supposed must have been Ober's Wisdom had brought the animal across to where Ober lay, had dragged the body on down in the direction of the roan, probably using a rope he'd found on Ober's saddle.

Next. Wisdom had paused close by the road for a considerable time—she supposed that the arrival of the surrey had halted him there—and during that interval had somehow managed to lift the body onto the horse. He had finally gone on from that spot to where the roan was tied, then had taken both animals across the road and up the far side of the timbered notch.

She set out now to follow the sign of the two horses, and shortly it took her over the north crest of the shallow ravine and down its far, steeper side. She came abruptly to a point along the rim of a deep wash where a twenty-foot shelf of earth had fallen away, taking down with it a golden-leafed aspen sapling. The caved-in bank had every appearance of having been undermined during the runoff of yesterday's storm.

Yet the tracks of the two animals led her to that point and

no further. It was as though they had stepped off the edge of the high bank onto the sloping mound of loose black earth below without having left their prints along its surface.

Puzzled, she rode up the wash to a point where the bank shallowed and she could ride down it. Coming slowly back toward the mound of fresh earth, she came upon the tracks of one horse, the roan's. They led her straight in under the tilted-over aspen. She circled the cave-in, her wonderment growing as she reached the wash's lower stretch without having picked up the sign of Ober's animal.

Suddenly she reined in, looking back at the earth mound. A chill ran through her, and with a shudder she knew what had happened to that other animal, and to Ober's body.

She left the place quickly, not letting her eyes go to the fallen away bank again. She followed the roan's sign upward, till it left the wash and cut through timber again. Then, a quarter mile beyond, where a shallow coulee troughed a level stretch, she came upon the spot where Wisdom had spent the night.

An odd surge of happiness mounted in her then at sight of the ashes of a small fire. Putting her hand to them, she found them still warm. Wisdom had rested here, perhaps eaten, and the freshest of his boot prints around the ashes no longer made the blurred pattern of tiredness they had along the slope below.

The thought that he was probably only an hour or so ahead of her pushed into the background the imponderables of the night. By the time she left the coulee her depression had vanished and she found herself looking forward to what was to come almost with a pleasurable excitement. She discovered now that she had faith in Wisdom being able to explain what had happened in a way that wouldn't damage her opinion of him. That opinion, regardless of his having killed Ober, was strangely to his credit, like her father's.

She hurried, taking chances on losing the sign of Wisdom's horse as it struck straight from his camp in the direction of the road. Several times she went on even though she lost sight of the familiar hoof marks. Then all at once she realized she had lost them.

Backtracking her gelding, she came upon the sign again within two hundred yards. It was something of a shock then to see that it had once more joined with the tracks of Ober's horse. For quite an interval this startling fact confounded her, until finally she left the saddle and knelt alongside the maze of hoof prints to study them more closely.

The answer to the puzzle came as she saw the shoe marks of Ober's animal not as sharply cut as those of Wisdom's. The night's damp air had melted their edges where they had packed the earth. It followed then that Ober had left this sign sometime yesterday or early last night on his way up the valley. But if he had been riding up the valley, how had it happened that he could meet Wisdom lower down?

Wisdom was following that sign this morning for some unfathomable reason, and as she followed in turn she was trying to understand still another puzzling facet of Wisdom's behavior.

Within half a mile she was passing on its downhill side a landmark she knew well, the tall, charred spike of a lightning blasted pine. It told her she was nearing George Durwent's place. The road lay to the other side of the solitary pine, to the north of it, and it struck her as being odd that Ober should have stayed off the road whenever it was he had come along here.

Shortly, the sign angled across open ground and into the scrubby stand of jackpine edging the west of Durwent's clearing. She came upon a spot where Wisdom had sat his horse for some minutes in an inexplicable halt. From there on the two sets of tracks led her straight in to the lower edge of the ten acre clearing in which sat Durwent's house and outbuildings.

She stopped there where the twin ruts of the weed-grown side road cut out of the trees, wondering how she was to explain her presence here to Durwent. How Wisdom had been able to ride so openly in sight of the house was also puzzling her. She looked across at the house, seeing then that no smoke was coming from the kitchen chimney.

She was beginning to wonder where Durwent might be when a sudden alert lift of the gelding's head took her attention. She looked the way the animal's head had swung.

A saddled roan horse was grazing at the clearing's upper edge near the corner of the root cellar behind the house. A man squatted on his heels beyond the animal. She knew who it was even before the black whickered, bringing the man to a quick stand with a swift gesture of hand to thigh.

Gladness and relief thinned that night-long mood of depression and uncertainty in her then, and all at once the grey morning became less cold and dismal.

She saw Rush Wisdom's hand come slowly away from holster, empty. She started toward him.

That strong surprise of seeing a rider at the clearing's lower edge had quickened the dulled throbbing in Wisdom's head to a fierce pounding, and now for a moment he closed his eyes against the pain, bleakly taking in the fact of Ann Ladd's presence here. Seeing her start this way over the pine-fringed meadow, his one thought was of keeping her at a distance from the root cellar.

He swung up into the saddle tiredly, for the long night had taken a lot out of him. He tried to be deliberate as he started out toward the girl, holding the roan to a slow walk so as not to betray the urgency he was feeling, half his mind still trying to put some sure meaning to what he had seen on that expanse of bare ground in front of the root cellar.

Until this morning his understanding of the past in its relation to Frank had been concise and clear, with Jesse Ober standing alone in whatever intrigue had cost Frank his life. Yet now his understanding was a complete muddle. His exhaustion was in some degree responsible for this. But he knew that, even alert, his mind would have been confounded. For Ober had been here last night, either before his first attempt at ambush, or before the second. He had furtively met and talked to someone here, probably George Durwent. It was even possible he had returned to the draw, to his death, as a result of that meeting.

Or so Wisdom had been thinking. Yet now it seemed neither logical nor believable that any man of Ann Ladd's choice could have had anything whatsoever to do with Ober's actions last night, let alone with the man's behavior of months ago.

Trying to convince himself of that, he found no pleasure at all in the prospect of this meeting with the girl. If she had last night been the one unpredictable element in his chances of leaving the country safely and unnoticed, her presence here now made her the one real threat to those chances.

That thought must have betrayed itself in his expression as he drew rein and let her ride in on him. For the beginning of a glad smile faded from her eyes as she studied him,

and when she spoke it was in a note of uncertainty. "You
... you're all right, Wisdom?"

He nodded. "Thanks to you. And maybe to plain luck."

"I didn't really have much to do with it, did I?" She took
in the exaggerated tilt of his wide hat then, adding dryly,
"Hardly anything at all, now that you've taken off the band-
age."

"You're wrong," he was quick to say. "I meant that. You
have my thanks." He sensed the inadequacy of his words and
continued awkwardly. "If you're here to see Durwent, he's
gone. Been gone for twenty minutes."

"But I'm not here to see George."

Warily, he asked, "Who then?"

"You." As she spoke that one word, her look reflected an
abrupt unmasked concern.

"Why me?"

"A woman's curiosity, I suppose. We both were worried
about you."

"We?"

"You needn't worry," she told him, catching the edge of
alarm in his tone. "At least not as far as dad's concerned."

His surprise at learning that it was her father he had
glimpsed beside her as the surrey came up the road last
night was overshadowed by the meaning he put to her last
words. "You mean you're my worry?"

"Shouldn't I be?"

It suddenly became all important that he should know
exactly where he stood with this girl, and he asked, "You've
been in to see the sheriff?"

"Not yet." ... She was looking past him toward the house
now ... "But why are you here? How can you ride straight
in on a place and risk being seen?"

"The black man's gone, too. Drove a buckboard down the
road early, better than an hour ago." Over a slight pause,
Wisdom surprised himself by finding an explanation to his
being here that might satisfy her. "Thought I'd pick up some
extra grub before I hightailed. I was goin' to leave the money
for it."

Her glance went to the slope down which he had ridden.
"You won't find much up there in the cold cellar."

"Didn't want to go to the house unless I had to," he said
in some relief, seeing that she was accepting his explanation.

"I'll get you something from the kitchen. Come along." And she put the gelding on past him toward the house.

Following, he was feeling a strong sense of frustration and confusion, knowing that he stood on uncertain ground with this girl. And shortly, as she dismounted close by the house's small rear stoop, it didn't help at all to have her look around at him and say bluntly. "How much or how little you tell me about all this is strictly your own affair, Wisdom. But I'd like to know more than I do now, which is next to nothing."

He weighed this plain invitation for taking her into his confidence and at once rejected it, shaking his head, drawling, "You wouldn't want to know any of it. If I get the breaks, this is the last you'll ever see or hear of me."

"Someone's bound to miss Ober," she reminded him. "A wolf or a coyote might get at him, dig him out. So dad and I aren't your only worries."

Once again her words had jolted him. "You know then?"

"About what you did with Ober? Yes. I've been tracking you since first light."

He let his breath go in a slow, tired way, asking miserably, "Why?"

"Why?" she echoed in outraged impatience. Then, strangely checking that brief outburst, she went on low-voiced. "I began to wonder. About a lot of things. About why dad says we must keep out of this. About my giving you the benefit of an awfully strong doubt."

Wisdom could think of nothing to say to this and he sat silent, realizing how foolish it had been to give way to his curiosity and follow Ober's sign here. He should right now be far up along the pass road, on his way out of the country, on his way out of danger.

Yet here he was, talking to the one person who personified that danger. Seeing the absurdity of the circumstance, he at the same time understood that for some unfathomable reason Ann Ladd was wanting to trust him, and also wanting some assurance that her impulse was sane, reasonable.

His instinct was to ride out of here without telling her anything. But, thinking back on those tracks printed against the black earth at the clearing's upper edge, he began wondering for the first time if he really could leave the country now and ever be dead sure of having paid off the debt for Frank in full.

That growing doubt, that indecision, swayed him to go against his instinct now; and he looked down at the girl to ask, "What is it you want to know?"

"Several things. First, how it happens you came here knowing two men so unlike you, two of the rottenest men in the country. Both dead now. One I know you killed. Maybe you killed the other, too."

He shook his head, his look utterly grave. "You're wrong there. Idaho was my friend. It would be better than an even bet that Ober cashed him in."

"But you had known them both before," she insisted.

"I had."

Admitting this much, Wisdom hesitated, wondering how much more he could tell her without risking anything. And it was then that she put him a deliberate question:—

"Would all this have anything to do with a man named Lockhart?"

Her words struck with such impact that for a moment he was caught off guard, dumbfounded. He knew he had betrayed his surprise even before she murmured, "So Lockhart does have something to do with it."

He tried to get a grip on his confused thoughts then, and failed, saying, "You know something. What is it?"

"Now we're getting somewhere, are we?" She could have put a barb in the question, though there was none. "What do I know? Not much. Only that John Cromer mentioned Lockhart's name along with Idaho's yesterday."

"How?"

"He said Lockhart and Idaho were in this country together last year. That it looked queer to him, a man like Lockhart siding an outlaw. It seems Lockhart had been to see him with a letter of introduction from some railroad. He was a—"

"A railroad!"

Ann nodded, eyeing him in a questioning way. "Yes, a railroad." She watched the startlement drain slowly from his face and shortly asked, "Now isn't it your turn to talk?"

"What more do you know?" came his toneless query.

"Only that Lockhart died soon after leaving here. John says they sent his brother to prison for the killing."

Wisdom took in what she said while still thinking of that other, that first insight he'd had of Frank's reason for coming to Longbow. "Why would a railroad send a man in here? Are they building the line up from below?"

"No. Dad's said nothing about it. He's one of the commissioners and would be the first to know."

"Then why was Lockhart sent in?"

Her shake of the head, her, "I haven't the beginning of an idea," stopped a hard lift of excitement in him. His thought that he had been on the verge of discovering something far more important than Frank having been in here working for a railroad was hard to thrust aside. Then, over his disappointment, he realized that this girl had told him these things straightforwardly and without keeping anything from him. And now his sense of fairness told him that he owed her some sort of an explanation in return.

He was wondering how to begin, how much he could tell her, when she spoke again. "You haven't said so, but you did know Lockhart, didn't you?"

"Yes." As an afterthought, he added, "Knew him well. And the brother."

She eyed him in a questioning way, waiting for him to continue. And shortly he told her, "It was Ober's story at the trial in Laramie that sent the brother to prison. Only one thing was wrong with the story. It wasn't true, any of it."

He took in her strong puzzlement, not giving her a chance to question him as he went on, "So I'm here trying to get the right story. First on why Frank was killed, second on why the brother should have been framed."

"But you ..." Ann Ladd checked whatever protest she had been about to make, looking up at him in wonderment to ask, "You're saying Lockhart was killed because he ... because..."

"Because of something he had run onto here," Wisdom drawled as she hesitated. "He knew something that cost him his life. The brother was on his way here to help him in whatever trouble he'd run into. That much I know. They killed Lockhart, then hung the killing on the brother to get him out of the way."

"They?"

Wisdom frowned in thought, absentmindedly reaching to shirt pocket for a sack of tobacco, then staring vacantly down at his hands as he began building a smoke. "They, I think," he said musingly, speaking more to himself than to her. "I'd know more if Ober hadn't tried the bushwhack, if I could've got to him and made him talk instead. But my hunch is he was in this with someone else, someone who was playin' for higher stakes than Ober would ever've dreamed of. Why they wanted Lockhart out of the way, what they were after, is something I don't know."

He realized he was voicing a possibility that had been only fragmentary until this moment. Yet it was one he could no longer ignore in the light of what he had seen up there at the root cellar. And now that his reasoning had gone this far, he carried it a step further, drawling. "But it's something I intend finding out."

"So you're not really on your way out at all," Ann said gravely.

The choice having been put to him so squarely, Wisdom had a moment's doubt over the meaning of his discovery of less than ten minutes ago. The doubt was strong; but stronger still was his stubborn resolve of not leaving here so long as any doubt remained.

He rolled the wheat straw cigarette smoothly, tightly now, saying, "That depends a lot on you, miss."

"On me?"

"Doesn't it? Or maybe on both you and your father. One word from either of you and I have the law after me."

"I see," she murmured, eyeing him in a judging way as she asked, "Isn't that asking a lot?"

"It is, miss."

She smiled oddly then, telling him, "Miss. The way you say it makes me sound very old. I'm Ann to my friends. And I ... well, this does make us friends, doesn't it?" Without waiting for him to answer, she went on, "Only one thing worries me. None of this is playing square with John Cromer."

"None of what? Not telling him Ober's dead when the man made two tries at me? Suppose you or I tell him about Ober and his trumped up story about Lockhart's brother now? How do we prove it? Ober talking would be the only proof that'd hold water."

Wisdom shook his head as he lit his smoke and tossed the match aside. "This thing was never clear from the beginning. Ober's gone, it's worse still. So I play out the hand alone or not at all."

The girl's eyes hadn't left his face, and now she said, "You haven't told me about Idaho yet. He was working for Jesse Ober. Yet you call him your friend."

"We'll never know about Idaho for sure. But one thing

I do know is that he wasn't in Laramie and couldn't have known who Ober was. He was to meet me here, and my guess is he wanted a place to hole up till I pulled in. Ober must have tied him in with Lockhart from something he did or said, then got rid of him."

"He was meeting you here? Why?"

"Because he thought a world of Frank Lockhart. Because he wanted to pay off for Frank as bad as I do."

"I see," Ann said gently. Then, with a baffled sigh, she went on, "So now that Ober's dead, I'm your only worry. Dad and I."

"That's about the size of it."

"You understand I'll have to tell dad all this don't you? He's driving to town this morning. To see the doctor, not Cromer. I should be getting back to talk to him before he leaves."

He nodded, nothing more. And now she looked around toward the kitchen door. "Will you want the things you said you were after now?"

"Not if I don't have to hit the brush." When she frowned, not understanding, he added, "There's nothing to stop me from going straight back to Longbow and staying there."

"Nothing but me." She gave him a rueful smile; and he noticed that she squared her shoulders as she added, "Go back then. And I . . . I wish you luck, Wisdom."

That morning, some two hours after Wisdom and Ann Ladd had left Durwent's place, a portly old man pushed his way through the swing doors of the *Fine And Dandy* in Longbow. Len Patch, the owner, saw who it was and glanced up at the clock. "You're late, Fred."

"Mud's still so confounded deep a man can hardly wade through it."

"She'll be deeper still before night."

"Looks that way." Fred Burke, Martha's father, laid half a dollar on the counter, shivering and rubbing his hands together as he glanced around to see that he and the saloonman had the place to themselves. "The usual, Len."

Patch set a quart bottle and glass before his customer, said, "Be with you in a minute," and walked on back to the rear of the room.

For all of a minute as the saloonman was working back there—unpacking glasses from a wicker hamper and blowing the sawdust from them—Burke's attention was apparently on the savoring of his morning whiskey. But presently, without turning his head, his eyes shifted furtively so as to observe Patch.

There was one four-second interval when the man's back was turned. And in that space of time Burke's hand darted to the counter's back edge, dipped into a box labelled, *Mule, Cut Plug, Fancy.* By the time Patch looked around again, the old man's hand had snaked to coat pocket, up again and was resting idly on the bar's edge.

The saloonman shortly sauntered back opposite Burke and ran his towel over the counter. "They tell me Martha had a front row seat at the fight yesterday, Fred."

"Couldn't get much out of her. She was there though."

"Now why couldn't it've been me?" Patch complained, reaching to the cash drawer and making change. "Think of it, that damn' mean grizzly finally gettin' whittled down! By the way, did Martha say was it this gent's right or his left got to Myrick?"

"Both, as I make out." Burke drained his glass, said nervously, "Got to hurry back, Len. See you around noon." He took his change then and started for the street.

A broad smile broke across Patch's loose-jowled face as the batwing doors swung shut behind the old man's back. He was still grinning as he glanced down into the box of plug and counted the black squares of tobacco there. Slowly then, his face went slack with wonder, the smile fading. He reached up and turned higher the lamp hanging above the bar. He counted the squares a second time, getting the same answer.

"Now when the hell could he've grabbed it?" he asked aloud, his deep voice echoing through the empty room.

Fred Burke made his rheumatic way from the saloon across the street to Kramer's, choosing carefully the spots where the mud was ridged and beginning to dry. He was stamping the mud from his boots when he noticed Ira, George Durwent's man, sitting alone on the bench close by to this near side of the store's doorway.

Ira's square, flat face at once shaped a broad smile that put a clean white gash across it. "How's pickin's, Mist' Burke?"

"Now Ira!" the old man said testily, straightening in a show of indignation. Then, because Ira's smile was so warm and friendly, so knowing, Burke decided not to take offense. He

even allowed himself an owlish wink, saying, "Not so bad
... Not at all."

He abruptly remembered a cigar he'd put in his coat pocket
late yesterday afternoon; and, because he neither smoked nor
chewed and knew Ira did both, he took out the cigar and
handed it across now. "Here, you look cold, boy. Light this
up."

Ira's look was both surprised and pleased. "That's right
kind of you, sir. You buy it?"

" 'Course I did." Burke's look turned briefly severe once
more before he asked. "What brings you in so early?"

"Letter to go out for the boss. Grub to haul and wheat to
get ground."

"Say hello to George." With a parting lift of the hand,
the old man entered the store.

Having just been reminded of a letter, Burke turned left
inside the door toward a head-high wire cage with a wicketed
window placarded, *Post Office*. The window was closed. He
glanced idly toward the rear of the merchandise packed room
to see Julian, Kramer's son, waiting on a woman at the far
dry goods counter. Except for those two, the store appeared
to be empty.

Casually, then, Burke stepped in between the post office
enclosure and an adjoining table piled high with work shirts
and overalls. He tried the cage's gate, found it open. He went
on in and took a sheaf of letters from the nearest pigeon hole
of a high rack, from the one marked, *Outgoing*.

He was leafing through the letters when he heard quick
steps coming from the store's rear, steps he could tell were
in a hurry. Excitement lifted in him, yet his hand was quite
steady as he took several letters from the bundle, ones he
hadn't even bothered to look at, and thrust them quickly
to the inside pocket of his coat.

Standing there, still thumbing one letter after another from
the bundle, he heard the steps close in behind him, heard
the grilled door squeal further open. Then a querulous voice
was saying:—

"Fred, you know no one's allowed in here!"

Burke turned. "Don't get your dander up, Sidney." With
a brief glance at the bespectacled, bald man who stood glaring
at him, he scowled down at the letters. "Dropped an invoice
headed for Junction down the outside slot last night. Made
a mistake on it. Where'd it go?"

"What time last night?" Sidney Kramer unceremoniously took the letters from Burke, returned them to the rack.

"After eight. After stage time."

"Stage was two hours late," Kramer said gruffly. "Your letter's gone."

"Hell!"

Burke stepped from the enclosure now, looked around briefly to say, "Thanks for the trouble, Sidney," and went out onto the street again, a secretive smile on his lined face that was observed, and partly understood, by the black man, Ira.

Sidney Kramer stood scowling darkly as his glance followed Burke out of sight through the window. He nodded perfunctorily to the woman customer as she left, turned then and walked on back to where his son was winding a bolt of yard goods.

"That old fool Fred was in the mail room," he said. "Found him sorting through some letters. Claimed he wanted one back he'd mailed last night."

"Maybe he did," Julian said.

"And maybe he didn't!"

"Well, Martha always brings back the things he swipes. I wouldn't worry."

"I'm going to tell her to keep him out of here."

"Tell Martha that? You wouldn't! Not as nice as she is. Is it her fault he's that way?"

The older man ran a hand over his hairless head, scrubbing it in exasperation. "After this, see you lock that mail room door, Julian. And keep it locked!" He trudged on over to his office.

From Kramer's, Fred Burke went straight on home. He was careful not to slam the yard gate in deference to Martha's insistence that he didn't need whiskey before the noon meal, and he took the side path on around the house to his shop out back. He hung his coat at the end of the work bench before he tied on a heavy canvas apron. Then he took up maul and chisel and began expertly chipping at the letter *K* he was carving in the name *Parker* on a granite headstone intended for the grave of a woman who had last week died in childbirth.

He had been working something under three minutes when the light on the stone faded abruptly. He turned and saw

Martha standing in the open doorway. At once he laid maul and chisel aside, reaching for his coat, remarking as he pulled it on. "Chilly. Soon have to keep a fire in here. Damn these early winters!"

She smiled knowingly and held out a hand. "What all did you come home with this time, pop?"

"Not a thing." He shook his head hard enough to bring loose strands of his thinning grey hair down onto his forehead. "Not a thing, I tell you."

Her hand remained outstretched. With a belligerent scowl he said, "Damn it, woman, I may be other things but not a liar! Get in to your housework and let me be!"

He never intended these outbursts as they sounded. Martha knew that as well as they both knew she would go through his pockets tonight once he was asleep. So there was no change in her smile now as she leaned against the door frame, telling him, "Don't be so grumpy."

"You're like your mother. Always pryin', always makin' a man feel he's tied to an apron!"

Martha's expression took on a quality of seriousness, though she had scarcely listened to his complaint. And now she said, "John was here for tea yesterday afternoon while you were gone, pop."

"Good." He beamed, thankful at a tender subject having been dropped. "You should have him often. There's a fine man."

"So I've been thinking," she said musingly. "He's almost too fine to treat the way I've been treating him."

"How's that?" His testiness returning, Burke tossed his maul angrily at the workbench; it struck the backboard, fell to the floor with a loud thud. "I've said this before and I'll say it again. This nonsense about me not living alone is childish. Your mother would turn in her grave if she knew what's behind it."

"Let's not talk about it, pop." Martha turned, pulling her shawl higher across her shoulders, about to leave.

"I mean that!" Burke blazed. "I won't be treated like a child any longer! You and John Cromer go on about your own affairs and let me look after mine."

"We'll see," Martha said softly. "We'll see." And she went out across the yard.

Fred Burke glowered at the empty doorway as he took off

his coat again. He stood there listening until he heard the slam of the kitchen door. Then, with a sigh, he picked up the maul, shaking his head as he straightened.

But as he went back to his work he gradually forgot the matter of Martha's mulishness and started thinking of something else. For some minutes then his mind was centered hard upon a game he and Martha had played for years, one her mother had played before her. It concerned various hiding places about the shop, the house and yard. Martha knew most of his favorites by now, the ash boxes of the stoves in summer, the eaves corners in the attic, even the loose rock under the cistern's lid. There probably wasn't one she didn't know.

Staring down at his stone as he pondered this, the stone itself suddenly gave him an idea. And a satisfied grin deepened the wrinkles at his eye corners.

His plan involved the use of two heavy wood blocks and a twenty pound crow bar. The execution of it took scarcely more than a minute. After the stone had been tilted, then eased down again on its platform, both the plug of tobacco and the letters he had taken from the post office, George Durwent's among them, were beneath it.

Matt Ladd's craggy face was set tight in anger as he reined his team into the Longbow road below Brush at ten-thirty that morning, at about the time Fred Burke was hiding the tobacco and letters under the stone. A cold, gusty wind was sweeping off the peaks, and Ladd found it in keeping with his mood as he went along thinking back over what Ann had told him this past hour.

A mile further on, the road made a bend around a big patch of jackpine. There Ladd came abruptly in sight of a roan horse standing at the road's edge. A man sat on a low outcrop alongside the animal, reins in hand. The man was Rush Wisdom.

Shortly, Ladd hauled the team to a stop abreast the roan, Wisdom at once sauntering in to the rig's near front wheel, saying, "Ann told me you were headed in to town. You ought to be back there where the doctor put you, sir."

"Be damned to that!" Ladd breathed, his glance sizing up this man in a way it hadn't yesterday.

"There are a couple things about Durwent I've dug up," Wisdom said then. "Things you ought to—"

"Ann's told me all of it," Ladd stated brusquely, adding, "Even more than you know."

He saw the look in Wisdom's deep blue eyes sharpen. "What more?"

"She'd left Durwent's place before she remembered how you'd been tracking Ober. So she went back."

Tiredness and a look of grim resignation showed strongly on Wisdom's lean face in that moment. "What did she find?"

"What you did," Ladd said bluntly. He continued in a grave tone, "It's too much for a man to take in. George being in with a tramp like Ober. Killing to get his hands on something he could've had for the askin'!"

A real alarm touched Wisdom's glance. "So the two of you have tied this in with the railroad wanting coal?"

"I have, she hasn't. It'd break her heart if she knew everything." A thought thinned the stern cast of the rancher's countenance then, and with a surprising gentleness he said, "You must be Lockhart's brother."

He could see his words strike Wisdom, could see the man's face blanching. And he was quick to put in, "Never mind. The less I know for certain the better. And I won't talk. Ann hasn't guessed it. But if you are the brother, your putting Ober where he is must mean a lot. If you're not, then Ober's still where he belongs. Now all that counts is making George talk. If he's what I—"

"You're going to try that?" Wisdom interrupted.

Ladd nodded. "Soon as I hit town. Ann says you saw him leave his place early, so town must be where he went."

Wisdom's look had lost its bleak quality of a moment ago. It seemed to Ladd that the man must have faced the bitter fact of his identity finally being known and was stoically accepting it; for now his glance took on concern and he shook his head, drawling, "You can't do it, sir. Suppose we're wrong about him. Where will that leave Ann?"

"How the hell could we be wrong?"

Wisdom shrugged, lifting a boot to wheel-hub as he looked up at the rancher. "Can't tell you how. But there's always the chance. And you'd never forgive yourself if you were wrong."

These two minutes of righteous anger, coupled with the aftermath of the rage that had been in him as he talked to Ann, were telling on Matt Ladd now. He could feel his heart pounding fiercely in the way that usually brought on that frightening, faint sensation of choking. "You want me to just let the whole thing go?" he asked in a purposely mild tone.

"No. You go at it a different way," Wisdom told him.

"Suppose you do see Durwent. But instead of havin' it out with him, tell him you're having a deed drawn up giving him and Ann title to that land off south you mentioned yesterday. Tell him you're doin' it for his own good."

"Wouldn't prove a thing."

"It would if he lost his head and tried to argue it. You're a good enough judge of a man to see how it hits him. If you see he's real sore, then there's plenty of time to throw what you know at him."

Ladd was gripped by a keen disappointment, for he had been hating George Durwent with a killing hate. Yet now the logic of Wisdom's argument gradually struck home to him, until shortly he could say, "Maybe it would be fairer to Ann that way."

Wisdom at once nodded and typically, Ladd thought, pressed his point no further. In this moment the rancher realized that the man had halted him in a reckless and headstrong act, one that might have meant heartache for Ann. And in gratefulness, the rancher said, "This ought to be the other way 'round, me doin' something for you. Is there anything I can do?"

"You can tell Cromer what you said yesterday you would."

"It'll be the first thing I do when I hit town."

Wisdom walked across to the roan now, swung into the saddle and brought the animal over alongside the buggy. "Another thing. How do I get to that coal pit of yours?"

Ladd frowned, looking off through the trees. "You can go straight north from here as far as the top of a rise that puts you in sight of the house. Make a quarter swing left, ride a mile and you'll be there. But how come you want a look at it?"

"To see how big it is."

"How big? Never thought much about that." Ladd looked soberly across at Wisdom then to say, "Better keep in touch with me, son. I'll be in town till late. Or you're welcome anytime at the house. More than welcome."

Wisdom nodded, lifted a hand, drawling, "Luck," and pulled the roan around, heading into the trees.

Over the next mile, Matt Ladd held the team in to a walk, deliberately weighing what he was going to say to George Durwent. It would call for a considerable amount of self control, and he had to keep reminding himself that he would be doing it for Ann, for his every instinct was to force a showdown with Durwent. But in the end he convinced himself that Wisdom's way was the better of the two.

Coming presently to the head of Spruce Ridge, he swung the surrey off through the thin pine growth, following wheel tracks that skirted the drop-off and led to the far, more gradual slope. It was while he was on his way down through the trees, the river lying close below, that he saw a rider coming toward him along the stretch of road opposite.

Anger began boiling in him the instant he recognized the man's rhythmic up-and-down style of sitting his animal's fast jog and he was thinking that no one but George Durwent rode a flat saddle in this country, that certainly no one but the Englishman ever sat leather any way but firmly.

By the time he was reining the team out across the muddy flats toward the crossing, he had put a strong grip on his anger and was giving Durwent the benefit of every doubt he could, even trying to convince himself that this was all a mistake, that there was a far different explanation than the one he had found to the nightmare of last night and this morning. Durwent was after all the man Ann had chosen. He was therefore incapable of this treachery.

Travellers along the road would usually stop along the gravelly shallows at the far side to let their animals drink. Ladd halted his team there out of habit. And it was there that he and Durwent met.

The Englishman, his smile as easy-coming and natural as usual, spoke the first word. "You're a sight for sore eyes, Matt! When did they let you up?"

"They didn't. Got up on my own," Ladd answered in his customary blunt manner. Then, without further preliminary, he spoke what was on his mind. "George, I've been wantin' to see you. I'm on the way in to catch up on some things I've neglected lately. Got to go to the bank, see to this new room they're puttin' on the church, and so on. Then there's that deed to you and Ann on that land. Think I'll have it drawn up."

There was a brief look of outright delight in Durwent's eyes before he quickly glanced away, pretending to ease the reins as his animal tossed its head. Then, as his horse began drinking once more, he eyed the rancher solemnly. "No hurry about it, Matt. None at all." His manner was oddly nervous and he laughed with an edge to his voice. "Fact is, I haven't been able to get Ann to name the day yet."

"She'll get around to that." A rising excitement brought on that constricted feeling in Ladd's chest then as he went on, "Now don't take this wrong, George. But I've decided on the strip off south instead of the chunk you want. Ann's the one to be pleased here, and that's still her choice."

He was eyeing Durwent closely and saw the instant alarm, then the look of suppressed fury come to the man's eyes. Durwent quickly hid that emotion, even smiled faintly. "Hadn't you better wait till I've talked it over with her again? This will change a lot of my plans."

"What plans are they exactly, George?"

Durwent's look of surprise told Ladd that he was playing his part poorly even as he sensed that his tone had been too deliberate, too pointed. And now Durwent's glance narrowed suspiciously. "Why should you ask? You know as well as I what they are."

"Look, George. This country's not ready for lumber and coal yet," the rancher said in a deliberate attempt at patience. "I've seen Pat Ruling's books. The man's makin' a bare livin'. As to the coal end of it, I doubt—"

"I intend to . . ." Checking his coldly-worded interruption, Durwent added more mildly, "I would like to see Ann before you proceed with this, Matt."

"Go ahead with what you started to say." Ladd's voice was again brittle with an anger he could no longer hold back. "You intend to what?"

"I was going to say that I intend managing my own affairs." Durwent was frowning in puzzlement as he gave his answer, obviously not understanding the rancher's testiness. Yet he was being careful now, and he added, "I'm a grown man, Matt My judgment should count in this."

"Judgment! The only trouble is your judgment's all bad!" The rancher spoke loudly, his anger getting really out of hand now. "Here I want to set you up for life, put you in the cattle busines; on a payin' basis! And you throw your chance away!"

The sight of Ladd's face turning livid, apoplectic, warned Durwent that he had gone too far in opposing the man. On the point of apologizing, an awesome thought struck him. He was realizing something that hadn't occurred to him until this moment. Very carefully he considered it. Then, in a deliberately brazen and taunting way, he said, "Better watch it, you fool! You're getting excited."

That warning was lost on Matt Ladd as he sat a moment

dumbfounded at this flagrant disrespect. Suddenly in a furious, slashing gesture, he threw the rein ends to the rig's floor lunging erect as he roared, "A fool, am I? You'll damn' well keep a civil tongue with me, you ..."

His rage seemed to drain him of strength, for his words broke off and he began breathing heavily as he glared at Durwent. And Durwent picked that moment to say coolly, "Watch it or you'll kill yourself!"

Ladd took a hard grip on the splash board with one hand, fisting the other as he bellowed, "Talk to me like that and I'll ... I'll ..."

"You'll do what?" Durwent asked coldly.

"I'll ..." Suddenly Ladd's two hands clawed, going to his chest with a hard, digging gesture as his face purpled in a blazing hate. But then he was staring wildly in stark fear, not at Durwent, not at anything as his jaw slacked open. He tore at his coat, ripped his shirt apart. Hoarsely dragging in one huge breath, he all at once slumped sideways and down onto the rig's seat.

The brief panic that had hit Durwent died out as he saw the stiffness go out of Ladd's frame, saw it go slowly limp. Sweat had broken out across his forehead, and now he took a clean white handkerchief from hip pocket and mopped his brow. He looked around, scanning the stretch of road he had just ridden, then the wind-ruffled reach of the river and the opposite slope. No one was in sight.

He put his horse closer in alongside the surrey. He leaned outward from the saddle and carefully, tenderly almost, felt of Matt Ladd's downhanging wrist.

He could feel no pulse beat. He smiled then in a completely satisfied way as he softly said, "It'll be that south strip after all, Matt. And all the rest along with it."

Five

THE STORM broke across the slopes below the peaks shortly
before eleven in a smother of heavy, damp snow. Within another twenty minutes its gusty, swirling onset swept down
upon the upper valley, until presently it was raining as it had
night before last, steadily, a downpour. And it was as the
downpour set in that Rush Wisdom slowly walked the path
leading from Brush's crew quarters toward the house.

He was still a trifle stunned, finding hard to believe what
he had come across there at the foot of Spruce Ridge half an
hour ago. His finding Matt Ladd lying lifeless in the surrey
as the team grazed so placidly at the side of the road held that
same quality of unreality as last night's waking nightmare.
And now, having helped two Brush crewmen carry the body
into the bunkhouse, he was on his way to see Ann.

Wisdom was feeling a strong sense of personal loss in Matt
Ladd's passing. Part of this was because the rancher's promise
of protection from the law had died with him. That sense of
aloneness, of being outlawed and hunted, had returned more
strongly than ever. But more than this was involved. He had
liked and respected Brush's owner, and felt he had lost a
friend. Furthermore, Ladd had been the one man alive who
had some insight to what he was trying to do here. The man
had been thinking as he did of the startling facts he had un-
covered this morning at Durwent's. Could Ladd have realized
that his coal pit was nothing but a mere gouging at the surface of a vast deposit, he would have been more than ever
convinced that his suspicions were real.

Wisdom had spent enough time with Frank on his various
jobs to have gained more than a little knowledge of geology.
It hadn't taken him long to realize the significance of what
he had seen shortly after leaving Ladd.

But now Ladd was gone. Wisdom had needed help in this,
and that help had suddenly been taken from him.

He wasn't looking forward to the chore that faced him now. Yet there had been no choice. The two men at the bunkhouse had been so stunned, so completely bewildered, that he had given in to their insistence that he be the one to see Ann.

Coming out of the trees and crossing the grassy stretch toward the house, he was struck by that same sense as yesterday of this being as pleasant a place as a man could wish to gaze upon. Lamplight glowed in two of the windows, cheery against the day's greyness. The mottled pattern of the vines climbing the weathered, square hewn logs, their deep green contrasting so strongly with the bright red patches where early frost had nipped them, gave the squat building a look of ripe age, of being well cared for. It was the smoke that lay heavy over the roof, coming from the big stone chimney and giving promise of the warmth and friendliness inside, that laid a deeper sense of despair through Wisdom, knowing as he did that the word he brought would lay a blight upon this home.

He was climbing the broad steps to the porch, staring dismally down in wonder over how to set about this distasteful task, when he heard the door open. He halted below the topmost step, the rain dripping from the brim of his hat, and looked across to see Ann standing in the doorway.

Lamplight from the room beyond strongly silhouetted her. She was wearing what she had been this morning, waist overalls and a heavy shirt that accented her slender shape, her tallness. And as he looked at her, trying to catch her expression in the poor light, he could only guess that there was a pleased welcome underlying her strong surprise.

"You, Rush!" she said in a way that let him know the welcome was there. "What's brought you? Come in."

Tiredly, he took the last step, unbuckled the stiff slicker and laid it over the porch railing. Then, with a sudden, angry sweep of arm, he removed his hat and shook the wet from it.

She must have caught some hint of what was coming from that gesture, and from the dead serious set of his lean face. For, as she took a backward step into the room to let him enter, her expression took on a slow alarm. "So you were the one driving the rig," she said. "Something's happened!"

He came in through the doorway, reaching around to close the door, feeling awkward, tongue-tied as he nodded. He swallowed thickly, trying to think of a way of lessening the shock for her, unable to. Then bluntly, quietly, he told her, "It's your father, Ann."

A momentary look of terror came to her hazel eyes. They brightened suddenly with tears. Then, their look softening, she breathed, "You needn't . . . He's dead, isn't he?"

Her glance held to his only long enough to catch his slow nod before her head dropped and she buried her face in her hands. For a long, uncomfortable moment he looked down upon her, watching the way her silent weeping made her shoulders tremble. Then, sensing how alone and miserable she was, he reached out and gently took her in his arms, pressing her head to his chest as he drawled, "Let it come, Ann."

His words made her sob brokenly, and she held herself rigid as she tried to keep back the outpouring of her grief. Then gradually he could feel the stiffness going out of her, and she wept unashamedly, relaxing in his embrace as though seeking the comfort of his closeness.

Presently she put her hands against his chest and turned her head into the bend of his arm, no longer crying. And for several minutes they stood that way, the quivering of her body and the catching of her breath subsiding as her emotion spent itself.

All at once she spoke, her voice calm, low with a deep sadness. "It's as though I'd been expecting all along it was coming, Rush. Without really knowing it. All I can think of is . . . is hoping it happened quickly for him."

"Couldn't have been any other way," he told her. "He was lying there on the seat of the rig, like he'd gone tired and stretched out to rest."

She pushed gently away from him now, her head bent as she put a handkerchief to her eyes. Then, looking up with a tenderness and a strong awareness of him, she murmured, "I hope he knows about this. About your being so good to me. He liked you, Rush."

He stood silent, knowing of nothing to say. And her glance dropped away from his as she said forlornly, "If only our last time together had been more pleasant."

"My fault."

"No, not yours," she was quick to say, looking up at him again. "Not yours at all."

What she had left unsaid made him feel awkward. Regardless of her denial, he was very conscious of having been the cause of the unpleasantness with her father this morning. But any further mention of this was pointless now, the burden of her worry being something he was wanting to lighten rather than add to.

So he picked this moment to say, "You'll want your friends to know about this. Who do I see besides Cromer?"

Her eyes took on a quick alarm. "You can't go to him!"

"Easy enough. What could he know?"

She said hesitatingly, "Then John is the one to go first of all. Leave the rest to him."

"You'd like him out here right away, wouldn't you?"

"Yes. And Martha. Have him bring Martha Burke if she can come."

He stepped over to the door now and opened it. But then he hesitated, looking back at her. "You'll be all right alone?"

She nodded slowly, in a way that let him know she had something else to tell him. And he didn't at all understand the faint anger that touched her glance just then, until abruptly she was saying, "Please tell John that there's to be no one else out here this afternoon. Tomorrow it'll be different. But not today."

It was plain to him that she was thinking of George Durwent, and he was longing to tell her of his talk with her father, of what they had suspected of the man. But he understood then that this girl already knew enough of Durwent to be doubting him, that nothing he could tell her beyond what she already knew was based on real fact.

"Call on me if I'm needed," he said.

"I would like you to be here tomorrow." She smiled now in a way that somehow gave this moment an intimate quality. "Thank you, Rush."

Her smile lingered in his mind's eye all the way to Longbow, shortening the miles, taking the dreariness out of the cold, wet day.

George Durwent had waited twenty minutes there near the river, holding his horse deep in the willows and waiting to make certain no stray rider had seen what had happened at the shallows. Afterward, he had struck back for town, avoiding the road, a fierce exultancy in him as he realized that the last remaining obstacle to his ambitions had been so miraculously removed.

It troubled Durwent not the slightest to think that he

had intentionally goaded Matt Ladd to fury, that he was directly responsible for the heart attack that had killed the man. Until today he had treated the rancher with considerable respect, had been very wary of him, long ago having postponed any guessing on what Ladd's attitude was to be when it came to dealing with the railroad on the coal. Now he would never have to face that worry, or the worry of having to convince Ann once again of his good judgment in the choice of the land they were to have as a wedding gift. The land was his now, along with the rest of Brush, or soon would be.

All this heightened his impatience over Jesse Ober not having shown up in town this morning as they had agreed he would. He had grown tired of waiting for Ober, had been on his way to Brush to satisfy his curiosity over Wisdom's visit yesterday when he'd had the unbelievable luck of meeting Ladd. Now it no longer mattered where Wisdom had gone yesterday, or why. All he needed was Ober's word on Wisdom to seal the certainty of a future, rich beyond his wildest imagining.

When the outskirts of Longbow lay in sight below, he cut across and rode an alley that paralleled the main thoroughfare, shortly turning down the first cross street. *The Union*, a run down saloon Ober frequented, lay close ahead now, and as he approached the place he put his horse onto the cinder path, pausing by the building's grimy window just long enough to peer into the dimly lit interior and make certain that Jesse Ober wasn't one of the three men he could see in there.

He slanted out into the street once more and followed it to the lower edge of town, until he was in sight of a shack where lived a woman of Ober's acquaintance who could be found in *The Union* most nights after dark. A blanket was hung over the shack's window, and no horse stood under the lean-to at the rear.

His impatience with Ober mounting, he rode back up to the main street, coming out of the saddle before Ennis's pool parlor as the lowering clouds were laying the first light curtain of rain over the town. He found Ennis's tobacco tainted room cold, deserted even by its owner, and in strong disgust he went back out to throw poncho over saddle and walk on down to Walt Heffran's for the midday meal.

Though he told himself there was no real reason for worrying, a suspicion was tightening in him that perhaps Ober had run into trouble last night. It was typical of him not to accept that suspicion just yet. He rationalized that, with Ober's mention of Horse Lake last night, it wasn't reasonable to expect the man to be back from a long ride to the peaks country, especially if he had camped after finishing his grisly chore. More important than being sure of Ober just now was the probability that any moment someone would be bringing him the news of Matt Ladd.

That word was longer in coming than he'd expected. He killed almost an hour over his meal, the better part of still another at the bank going over his accounts. This last interval would have been an exceedingly unpleasant one but for the fact that the future held the almost immediate prospect of affluence; for one of his notes for three hundred dollars was within a week of being due, and his cash account was alarmingly low in the two figure bracket.

It was as he left the bank that John Cromer hailed him from across the street.

He knew at once from the serious set of the law man's face what was impending. And as Cromer solemnly gave him the news, he was more intent on making his grief appear genuine than he was in listening to the particulars.

But suddenly one word Cromer had spoken several secconds ago finally penetrated the armor of his guile. And involuntarily he burst out, "You said Wisdom? He's in town?"

Cromer halted in mid-sentence, a frown wrinkling his forehead. "That's right, Wisdom, the one that—"

"I know, I know," Durwent interrupted for the second time, this time with an impatience he couldn't control and was at once regretting. Then, knowing he had betrayed a great deal more of his feelings than he was accustomed to, he tried to smooth over the matter by saying, "A hell of a thing, isn't it? Matt dying that way and then being hauled around by a complete stranger."

"Don't see as it makes much difference who brought Matt in," Cromer drawled, pointedly, eyeing him in a puzzled way. "When a man's dead, he's dead, George. Besides, what's wrong with Wisdom?"

"Nothing. Not a thing," Durwent said hurriedly. Then, shrugging, he went on, "I'll have to get right out there."

The law man gave him an odd, puzzled look. "You weren't listenin', George. I was just sayin' Ann asked not to have anyone come to see her this afternoon. Just me and Martha. Better wait till morning."

Durwent bridled on two counts now, the first being that he didn't like Cromer telling him what to do, the second that he had let this news of Wisdom bring his guard down before the sheriff. And, before he could reconsider, he was saying testily, "I'm going regardless. Ann would certainly want me."

Cromer's jaw set hard. He seemed on the point of arguing the matter. But then, with a lift of brow, he apparently changed his mind, saying only, "Suit yourself. It's your affair, George."

Afterward, watching Cromer go back up the street as his mind tried to take in what Wisdom still being alive meant, Durwent doggedly held to the decision that he was going to Brush this afternoon. But before he started his third long ride of the day, he had to know more about Wisdom.

It was this thought that started him obliquely across the street toward the *Exchange* before he quite realized his purpose. He had to find Wisdom, for what particular reason he hadn't decided yet. But something had to be done about the man.

The high running excitement of these past three hours since leaving the river was dying in him as he understood that Wisdom had replaced Matt Ladd in standing in the way of his ambitions. And in trying to think of what he should do about the man, it was typical that he had already dismissed Jesse Ober from mind, the certainty that Ober was dead rousing no more emotion in him than he would have felt on learning of the death of a stranger. He had always looked on Ober as being one of that breed of lesser men destined to be used by their betters, then cast aside and forgotten. Perhaps it was really a stroke of luck for him that Ober was out of the way, the man having represented the only link to a past Durwent wanted kept hidden.

But Wisdom was just as sure a link to that past. He would have to go the way Frank Lockhart had gone, along with Idaho and now Ober. According to John Cromer, Wisdom was in town. The hotel was the place to start looking for him.

He found George Hardy at the desk in the *Exchange's* lobby. With a forced affability, he greeted the man by saying,

" 'Afternoon, George," and was answered, " 'Afternoon, George."

They both smiled over the performance of this ritual that was much the same each time they met. Hardy was one of the very few people in this country who ever called Durwent by his given name, allowing himself this familiarity only because Durwent had patronizingly invited it.

But now Hardy's smile quickly faded. "It's hell about Matt, George. There went a good man."

"One of the best," Durwent agreed with a solemn nod. Then, breathing a long sigh, he went on, "I'm trying to find Wisdom. Understand he's in town."

"He is. Right up in his room."

"Which one is it?"

"Eight. Front north corner. But you'll find him dead to the world, George. Said when he come in he felt like sleepin' a week."

Durwent showed his surprise. "What's wrong with him?"

"Y' got me. Part of it might've been his runnin' onto Matt the way he did. But it looked like more'n that. Like he'd been with a bottle all night. Or maybe rode a long ways."

Durwent deliberated a moment, finally saying, "I can see him later," and left the counter to go back out onto the street.

For the first time he began wondering if he hadn't been hasty in his judgment of what had happened to Ober. Wisdom coming so openly back to town, sleeping in a hotel room, hardly indicated that he had last night killed a man. But, regardless of whether Ober was living or dead, something had to be done about Wisdom.

He paced slowly along the walk past the courthouse, shoulders hunched to keep the back of his neck from getting a wetting as he rejected first one idea then another on what to do about Wisdom. His thoughts were mixed up now, he felt at a loose end. By the time he had reached the shelter of Elder's Market's leaky wooden awning, his aimless walk had slowed. Finally he stopped, trying to decide what next to do. He had some stray notion of wanting to stay in sight of the hotel, though he had no notion at all of what he would do if Wisdom appeared.

Idly, he looked back past the courthouse and the store beyond to the *Exchange*, his glance going to the corner window above the veranda. He noticed how the adjoining store's flat roof came against the hotel wall some three or four feet below the corner window. And in that moment he was really wishing that Ober could be here to earn the bills of sale he had pocketed last night. But then he knew that even Ober wouldn't risk what he was thinking of, and he thrust the idea aside irritably.

He had turned and was walking slowly toward the corner when he saw Ira drive the buckboard out of the cross street and turn his team this way. Sight of his crewman in town so late in the day at once roused his anger, and he went to the walk's edge and stood there waiting.

Ira saw him and reined the team over alongside the near rail, his face wearing a sallow, yellowish cast that was eloquent of this bitter weather's effect on him. Then, before Durwent could speak, the black man was saying miserably:—

"That poor Matt Ladd, boss! Gone, they tell me."

"He is, Ira."

"If ever a man went to sit beside the good Lord, it's him."

Durwent ordinarily had little tolerance for his man's deep religious feelings. Now he had none at all, and said dryly, "You'll be right up there with him if you don't hustle on home. This is a poor time of day to be starting a twelve mile trip."

"Couldn't help it, Mist' George. They was fixin' the wheel at the mill and just got my wheat ground."

Durwent had the impulse then to mention something he had time and again tried to drive home to Ira, the fact that the man was fast losing the correct speech he'd been trained to and was instead speaking like the commonest brush jumper. But just now a gust whipped along the street, throwing a fine spray against his cheeks, and impatiently he said, "All right, get along then. Did you get the letter here in time?"

Ira nodded. "Stage was late again." His look saddening, he asked, "You reckon they'd mind if I went to the buryin', boss?"

Durwent's glance had a moment ago gone out onto the street, to a freight pulled by a three team hitch. And now as he casually thought of the freight probably being one of Myrick's, an idea suddenly struck him. The next moment he realized Ira was waiting for an answer, and he said, "Better not, Ira. Your kind has no place among white people."

"But old Matt was my friend, boss. So's Miss Ann."

"No, I said!" The black man's talk was unwelcome now, engrossed as Durwent was in thinking of something else. And he added just as sharply, "Get along home."

He wasn't aware of the hurt in Ira's face, even of the buckboard's pulling away, as he stood there watching the big freight pulling slowly down the street, thinking of Myrick. An expression of wonderment, almost of eagerness, crossed his face. Then he smiled.

Presently, after his thinking had taken on a definite pattern, he walked on down to Kramer's store, on his way seeing John Cromer and Martha Burke going out the street in one of Arnholt's hired buggies. Thus reminded of his decision to ride to Brush, he began hurrying.

Kramer senior was in the post office cage and at once spoke in his ingratiating way, offering his sympathies on Matt Ladd's death.

Durwent accepted the man's words as graciously as he could, then asked, "Any mail for me?"

Kramer looked in the rack, shook his head. "None yet. You could stop in at eight when the northbound's due. If you're still around."

"I'll do that." Turning from the window, Durwent abruptly stopped, looking back at the man as though he'd just thought of something. "By the way, what truth is there to this story I've been hearing about Myrick?"

The store owner frowned. "What story?"

"About his backing out of a chance to fight Wisdom."

Kramer's face went slack with surprise. "That can't be! Only last night he was at Len Patch's boastin' how he'd pay money for another chance at Wisdom."

"Well, let's hope it's not true. But I've heard it twice and there must be something to it. And here I was ready to place my bets on him."

"Me, too," Kramer said worriedly. "Well, I'm damned!"

Before he left town at four o'clock, Durwent had engaged in two more conversations remarkably like the one with Kramer. One was with Harrison Elder, the market owner, the other with Walt Heffran.

The day's wan light was fading into a murky dusk by the time he sighted the lights of the Ladd house glowing at the top of Brush's long meadow. And as he turned up the forks toward the layout, he was reminded of how the place had awed him in the old days. Countless times he had traveled this stretch of road feeling shut out, envious, wondering at the grand life that must be lived in the big log house at the top of the hill. But a year's close acquaintance with the Ladds had changed all that. Now he could be slightly scornful of the life lived there, of its pattern so closely following that of almost every ranch, big or small, he knew.

He saw it as an odd fact now, but nevertheless one that couldn't be argued, that most people here in western America knew little and cared less of the graces involved in having achieved wealth and social standing. Matt Ladd had been as common in both dress and manner as most of the men who worked for him. And Ann was just as common in some ways.

This unsettling realization had come to him frequently of late, and it was disturbing. Without yet having quite admitted that it mattered, he had begun wondering just what his family and friends would say if they knew of the match he was making. The people of this country, Ann included, were beneath him in many ways.

Riding in along the lane with the house in plain sight now, his unsettling and aloof thoughts of Ann faded as he tried to picture the changes that would soon be made here. In his mind's eye he could see a low rock wall and a small gate house at the foot of a real lawn instead of the present yard's expanse of wild, untrimmed grass. He would insist on a new rail fence around the pasture, painted white. Of course it would be a year or more before he could begin replacing the primitive log structure of the main house with a more suitable one of brick, hewn timbers and quarried granite.

He thrust all this from his mind now as he rode up on the house, exerting a definite strength of will to force himself into the somber mood he knew he must be in to face Ann. He tied his horse below the steps, threw his slicker over the saddle and hurried up onto the porch to save himself a wetting. His pulse quickened when, after his knock, a light step sounded in answer from inside.

But it was Martha Burke, not Ann, who opened the door to him. Her eyes were red and her expression utterly grave as she said in a hushed tone, "Come in, George. We'll have to be quiet. Ann's asleep."

"Do her good," he said as he came in past her. "How is she?"

For a reason he didn't understand, Martha avoided his glance as she answered, "Exhausted. John and I thought we would let her sleep straight on through the night if she will."

Durwent had been about to hang his hat on the deer-horn rack by the door. But now, abruptly faced with the prospect of spending the evening with Martha and John Cromer, neither of whom he particularly liked, he hesitated. For a certain reason he didn't want to remain here too long, it being important that he should be in Longbow before the evening was well along.

So now, smiling in a way he hoped conveyed an impression of sorrow, he told Martha, "Then I'll just be in the way if I stay. Think I'll be going on. Is there anything I can be doing?"

Martha's relief was plain as she at once answered, "Nothing just now, George. John's seeing to most of it. He's down at the wagon shed now helping build the coffin."

"How about tomorrow? When would Ann like to have me here?"

"She didn't ... I would suppose ten o'clock would be early enough. People will be arriving by then."

Durwent nodded, favored her with his easy smile once more, and went on out the door, saying, "It's good of you and John to help, Martha. Ann and I will never forget it."

"It's little enough to be doing."

On his way out the lane, Durwent was wondering if anything but shyness had backed Martha Burke's slightly unwelcoming manner. In the end he decided it had been nothing but that alone. The woman was queer in some ways, timid and scornful of men, proof of which lay in her never having managed to catch herself a husband.

So thinking, he settled down to the long ride back to town, his thoughts once again turning to Wisdom, and to Ray Myrick.

Ann, lying on the bed in her room, listened with relief to the closing of the door as Durwent left the house. His steps crossing the porch laid faint echoes against the murmur of the rain on the roof, and then she knew he was gone. She hadn't liked having to ask Martha to see him, to make excuses for her that were at best only half truths. But Martha had been the one to urge her to lie down until supper was ready, after those trying minutes with John Cromer.

John was taking over for her, seeing to the digging of the grave alongside her mother's on the knoll behind the house, seeing to the building of the coffin. He and Martha would stay here tonight and between them manage things tomorrow when dozens of people would be calling to pay their last respects to Matt Ladd's memory.

So there was little she had to think of beyond the trial of the funeral itself. She had kept her father's accounts, had helped him make many decisions on the running of the ranch. Everything was in order, for his affairs had been hers. She had no material worries, none at all. And as she had tried to tell Rush Wisdom this morning, it seemed that she had long ago unconsciously prepared herself for Matt Ladd's death. The heartache was there, but without that sense of having had her world shattered.

Strangely enough, there was an odd and contrary feeling of contentment in her, one that was quite remote from her sense of loss. She had first been struck by it as Wisdom held her in his arms this morning. And now as she lay staring out the window across the rainswept, darkening hills, she tried to understand it. Perhaps Wisdom's gentleness, the soothing quality of his manner, had told her that what was happening was less tragic than sad. But that alone didn't account for this strange sense in her of being so at peace.

It was as her thoughts stayed with Wisdom in a somehow warm and exciting way that she was suddenly struck by the complete change the day had brought to her whole outlook. Matt Ladd's dying was partly responsible for this. But only partly. It was her way of thinking of George Durwent that had changed so.

There was in her makeup a large measure of her father's intolerance of anything halfway understood. Deliberately, trying to give Durwent the benefit of every doubt, she tried now to summon her old warmth of feeling toward the man, and failed. She was not only relieved at not having had to see him tonight, she was actually dreading their next meeting. What she had seen this early morning on riding back to the clearing's upper edge that second time, after Wisdom had left it, had turned to dead ash the blaze of her affection for Durwent.

She knew now with an abrupt and stark finality that she

no longer loved the man. She doubted that she could ever again trust him. She was condemning him without giving him the chance of defending himself, yet it simply couldn't matter what his explanation might be. For he had met Jesse Ober secretly last night, and that in itself condemned him.

Looking back over the past weeks, months even, she could see that her father and some of her friends, John Cromer particularly, had always disliked Durwent but had hidden their feelings out of respect for her. Even Wisdom, a stranger, had tried to save her hurt and humiliation this morning by taking particular pains that she shouldn't see those telltale boot prints and the tracks of Ober's horse there by the cold cellar.

She realized that all day long she had unconsciously been basing her judgment of Durwent on Wisdom's actions this morning, and on Matt Ladd's. She resented Durwent being responsible for making her last glimpse of her father a disagreeable one. Matt Ladd had been furious, outraged at the story she brought him about Durwent, unaccountably so. It had been his nature to reserve judgment on such a serious matter until he knew all the facts. Yet this morning he hadn't reserved it. It had seemed to her almost as though he suspected something of Durwent that hadn't occurred to her.

But all these shadings of emotions in others, these half-guessed truths about Durwent, were only faint shadows against the glaring fact of her changed feelings toward the man. And, queer as it might be, she felt relieved. A restlessness and a dissatisfaction she hadn't known was in her was gone.

She knew now that she could never marry George Durwent.

It was some minutes after this sobering realization had come to her that she heard John Cromer's voice, and another man's, sounding excitedly from the other end of the house. She sat up, listening, and shortly heard a man's heavy stride crossing the living room toward her door.

She called, "Come in," even before whoever it was could knock.

The panel swung open on Cromer's thin shape. The lamplight from the room beyond let her catch a hint of the dead serious set of his face, and at once she was asking, "What's happened, John?"

"Nothing for you to worry about," he was quick to say.

"But Ira's here. Scared half out of his wits. He was on his way home when he ran across a spot along the road above that's washed out. On his way around, he came onto Jesse Ober lyin' buried in a gulch that's flooded. Thought I'd—"

His words broke off and his glance sharpened. Then he was asking, "What's come over you, kid?"

"Nothing." Ann felt the color draining from her face as a stark fear for Rush Wisdom struck through her. Though she tried to keep her voice even, it broke as she went on, "I only ... It's just that so much has happened today, John. Now this."

"Sorry it had to happen just now, but I'll have to take some men and go dig Ober out. May be gone most of the night. But Mart's here to be with you."

"We'll be perfectly all right, John. Go on. Of course you'll have to take care of this."

The story reached Ray Myrick third-hand. His hostler brought it when he came back after supper to help ditch the mired wagon lot. The man found Myrick up to his knees in a water filled trench, a lantern sitting nearby on an upended box.

Finally, after Myrick had listened to the story and then questioned the man profanely, he pitched his shovel into the mud, waded out of the trench and said, "Stay with this. I'll be back." Five minutes later, having changed out of his gum boots, he slammed out of the gate shack and headed up the street.

That was the beginning of something he couldn't have foreseen, a thing Durwent had suspected might happen. He went straight to the *Fine And Dandy* and over his first whiskey sourly blamed Len Patch for having repeated the story. They exchanged some salty words, which ended as Myrick laid money on the counter for a full bottle.

Over the next hour and a half, Myrick handed out upward of a dozen drinks, each time having one himself as he treated a man and put him straight on how he really felt about fighting Wisdom. "Hell, I'm beggin' for a chance at him!" was a comment he made repeatedly, convincingly even after he was sodden with drink. His bottle was empty by the time George Durwent finally eased in alongside him, quietly asking:—

"Why the celebration, Ray?"

Myrick poured out his woes as freely as he had the whiskey, Durwent listening without once interrupting. Only when the big man had run out of words and was resting his swollen jaw in the palm of a hand, elbow on the counter, did Durwent casually observe, "Of course it must be Wisdom who started the talk."

Myrick reared erect. His whiskey dulled thoughts considered the statement, its inference being something that hadn't yet occurred to him. At length he shook his head. "Not Wisdom. It's someone else workin' off a grudge against me."

Durwent lifted his shoulders noncommittally. "Believe what you want, Ray."

Myrick leaned heavily on the bar once more, his brooding glance vacantly on the empty bottle before him. He noticed when Durwent turned away, about to leave, and he reached out to put a hard grip on the man's arm. "You really think so?"

"Would I have said it if I didn't?"

Myrick cocked his head, staring blearily across at the man. "Wants to stir up trouble, does he?" Straightening, he hitched up his trousers. "Well, he's gettin' it! From me. Right now! Where is he?"

"Better wait till you're steadier, Ray."

"Who says I ain't steady?"

Durwent shrugged again, reached over and tried to pull Myrick's fingers from his arm. But the big man's grip tightened. "Where'll I find this four-flusher?"

"I wouldn't know. But you could start looking at the hotel." Shaking his head, his look touched with pity, Durwent softly added, "And if you're serious about this, Ray, I'd take a gun along. Do you have one?"

Myrick let go the other's arm and pulled his coat open, patting the handle of a .45 Colt's wedged in his belt against hipbone. "Got one. And she's hair trigger, by God!"

"Loaded?"

"Why the hell wouldn't it be loaded?" Myrick asked. Deliberately then, he drew the gun and aimed it at the floor.

The shot deafened Durwent. He quickly drew back a step as Len Patch hurried up on the other side of the counter and laid a double-barreled shotgun in line with Myrick, bawling, "Put that away or I blow you in two! What the hell goes on?"

Myrick gave the shotgun and the man a placid stare, realizing the room had gone dead quiet. He thrust the Colt's back in his belt. Then, loudly, he announced, "Anyone wants t' have some fun, tag along with me!" And he pushed away from the bar to start walking unsteadily for the doors.

Patch asked, "What got into him, Durwent?"

The Englishman shrugged. "Says he's going after Wisdom. But I don't want any part of it."

There were a few other customers who felt as Durwent did. But a good many more at once made for the street on Myrick's heels.

George Durwent didn't seem to be in much of a hurry to finish his drink. But he left the *Fine And Dandy* at about the time he judged the crowd and Myrick would be reaching the hotel.

Rush Wisdom had been lying awake some minutes when he heard voices and the tramping of boots echoing up off the street. He lay there paying the sounds little attention as he stared up into the darkness relishing the warmth of the blankets against the room's chill he could feel at his face. He felt fine, completely rested. He was looking forward to a meal. There was only a faint smarting and a stiffness above his temple to remind him of the bullet gash.

This quiet interval had let him look back over last night and today and see certain things with a new, sharper perspective. Frank had been sent here by a railroad to look for coal. It was George Durwent, not Ober, who had first tried to bribe Frank and then, failing, had either killed him or had him killed. What had happened afterward in Laramie, particularly the false testimony at the trial, had taken a brain like Durwent's to think out.

He had nothing but his brief meeting with the man, and what Matt Ladd had said of him, on which to base his sureness that Durwent was thoroughly capable of this entire deception. Yet, though he saw it was quite possible Durwent had possessed some obscure foreknowledge of the worth of Matt Ladd's coal pit, he found it harder to believe the man capable of cold blooded murder. Ober was a far surer bet on having been the killer, not only of Frank but of Idaho. His own experience of last night backed this hunch on Ober. It followed that Durwent had either hired Ober, or blackmailed him, into the killings.

After his talk this morning with Matt Ladd, Wisdom had spent a good hour in the saddle that had left him considerably awed. The primitive workings at Brush's coal pit had scarcely touched a deposit so extensive that it tried a man's comprehension. From the pit he had ridden a mile in one direction, then a like distance in the opposite, to see ebony ledges continually thrusting through the thin topsoil of a long slope climbing fully a thousand feet to the higher tableland forming Brush's choicest graze. And afterward he had soberly understood what a temptation this might represent to any man.

What he didn't understand was what he should do now that he was sure of Durwent being the man he had come here to find. In one way he was less sure of himself than at any time since the end of his first hour in Longbow. His being a wanted man, the fact that there might even be a reward out for him, made little difference. What made him so unsure of what to do now was the thought of Ann Ladd.

This morning he had sensed that Ann's faith in Durwent had been tried almost to the breaking point. But in the hours since then it was quite possible Durwent had seen her, had managed to make some seemingly logical explanation about his meeting with Ober last night. He might not only have restored her faith in him, but strengthened it.

Wisdom's feelings toward Ann right now were different from yesterday's. Then he had been only slightly uneasy over what her opinion of him might be should she find out what he was doing for her father. Yet now her opinion mattered a great deal. In fact, he was soberly aware of it mattering so much that the settling of the score for Frank had become almost a secondary thing. He felt strangely powerless to bring on a showdown with Durwent so long as Ann still believed in the man. The cautioning word he had given Matt Ladd this morning, that of Ladd being certain he wasn't taking away Ann's chance for happiness, had become one he was giving himself now.

This was something new in Wisdom's experience. Never before had his emotions swayed him to ignoring good judgment, danger, even his allegiances. Yet his feelings toward this girl were driving him to do just that. The memory of that interval this morning when he and Ann had been so close, so wholly aware of nothing but each other, was as clear and alive in his memory as though it had ended only a moment ago. Their embrace had lacked all but the remotest quality of any physical awareness. Yet now as he looked back upon it, that awareness was strong in him. And he realized with a deep longing that this girl was infinitely desirable.

Yet his thoughts of her ran deeper than just the physical longing. They had more to do with those qualities he'd seen in her yesterday. There was a rightness about her thinking, a steadfastness about her. Her mind was alive and quick. All these things, along with the mischievousness he'd finally managed to rouse in her, told him that she was a woman who would one day make some man's life full and rich. She was a person of intense loyalties, of strong opinions. He had never much respected the opposite in anyone.

It occurred to him that George Durwent might after all turn out to be the man who was to share Ann's life in the years to come. By some freak of circumstance, Durwent might yet be proved innocent of the things he now seemed guilty of. Out of consideration for Ann, Wisdom conceded that quite honestly. But, aside from that remote possibility, his attitude toward the man was strangely lacking the rage and the fierce urge to destroy that had been in him when he faced Ober last night. The only emotion he could rouse was a strong contempt of Durwent, backed by the sober conviction that he would one day probably kill him. But because of Ann, that day might be longer in coming than he'd reckoned. It wouldn't come until, and unless, her feelings toward Durwent had changed completely.

The sound of voices from below, from the lobby, intruded on his thoughts now. He threw back the blankets and swung his feet to the floor, tightening his belt and then reaching down to pull on his boots. Afterward, striking a match, he had to shield the flame in his cupped hand against a stirring of damp, cold air coming from the room's corner window. He had lit the lamp and was at the washstand, pouring water into the basin, when he idly noticed a tramping of boots as several men mounted the stairs.

His curiosity not even faintly roused, he sloshed water over his face, dried it and then ran a hand across his unshaven cheeks, deciding to wait until morning for a shave.

Then suddenly a wariness lifted in him at hearing men coming along the hallway toward the front of the building. He glanced across at the shellbelt and holster hanging from the bedpost.

He had taken one step toward the bed when all at once a fist slammed hard against the panel of his door. An instant later the door burst inward and Ray Myrick's massive bulk stood in the opening.

The big man held a Colt's lined into the room. It swung slightly now, aimed at Wisdom as he halted almost within armreach of the bed. Myrick's glance settled on the weapon there, and with a jerk of the Colt's he said, "Back up, mister!"

Wisdom noticed the swaying of the man's upper body, how he stood with boots spread wide. He saw that the hammer of Myrick's .45 was drawn back and, very carefully, he edged out from the bed.

Myrick drawled thickly, "He decided not to, boys."

Wisdom could see four or five others in sight out along the hallway as Myrick moved into the room now. Then Myrick's swollen mouth was shaping an arrogant smile, and he said, "Guess we can settle this by ourselves," as he reached behind him and threw the door shut with an explosion that rattled the window's open sash.

"Now, Wisdom, let's hear you say it to my face!"

"Say what?" Wisdom spoke mildly, knowing the other was drunk.

"What you been sayin'. About me bein' scared to step into a ring with you!"

Wisdom moved his head in a spare negative. "That couldn't be, Myrick. Because I've never said it, because I don't believe it."

"Y' don't believe what?" Myrick asked belligerently, irrationally. "That I'm spooked over—"

"I don't believe you'd turn down a fight," Wisdom cut in. He went on good naturedly then, "They've put the shoe on the wrong foot, whoever they are. I'm the one that turned down the fight."

Myrick's look was startled. "Hear that, boys?" he called loudly. Then, his glance narrowing, he asked in a lower voice, "Y'did? When was this?"

"Yesterday. Durwent had the idea of matchin' us."

"Then whyn't you let him do it?" When Wisdom only

shrugged, an ugly, scornful look crossed the man's puffed face. "Y' know damn' well why! Y're lily livered! Now y' got the gall to spread it I'm the one!"

Wisdom was saying mildly, "Have it your way," when Myrick suddenly made a lunge for him.

The man's move was unexpected, a complete surprise. Somehow in his alcoholic state Myrick had been cunning enough to hide his purpose. He even moved first to one side, then the other, as he came forward, blocking Wisdom into a corner of the room.

Myrick lifted the Colt's as he closed in, bringing it down in a chopping, swift arc which Wisdom barely managed to avoid. The momentum of Myrick's move carried him off balance so that he lurched past Wisdom toward the bed, toward the window.

A shot that instant blasted from the front of the room, drowning out Myrick's grunt as he tried to catch himself. The deafening thunder of it caught Wisdom wheeling in behind the man, lifting a fist to hit him behind the ear.

Myrick's hoarse scream of agony came the next instant. His .45 fell from his hand as he clawed at his chest. And as his Colt's struck the boards it sent a second explosion thundering across the room's narrow confines.

The door burst inward as Myrick sprawled heavily across the bed. Then someone behind Wisdom was saying:—

"Make one move and you're dead as he is, Wisdom!"

Six

JOHN CROMER, dozing on the seat of the buckboard, roused at the echoes of two shots, one louder than the other, sounding faintly up from the town that lay less than a quarter of a mile below. His thought, *More trouble?* he at once answered by telling himself, *The hell with it!* Nevertheless, he slapped the team to a faster jog.

He was almost as dead beat physically now as he had been mentally since mid afternoon, since learning of Matt Ladd's passing. It had taken him and Ira, and a Brush crewman, better than an hour of backbreaking work to dig Ober out of the flooding wash below the cutbank. They had worked knee deep in mud and water through a steady downpour. And now Cromer was chilled clear through after this jolting, wet drive down out of the high country, his spirits little improved by the knowledge that Ober's stiff shape lay behind him in the rig's bed. With what was in prospect for him tomorrow, his temper was at its rawest edge.

He was on his way across the first intersection, the one above the *Exchange*, before he noticed a light shining from one ground floor window of the courthouse. It was his office window, and he took in that fact with a sober resignation.

Leaving the buckboard at the rail, he went on into the building's dark hallway to see the door of his office standing open. As he was on his way to it, a low mutter of voices sounding from the room beyond broke off.

He entered the office to find Walt Heffran, Harrison Elder and George Durwent grouped about his desk. It was Heffran who unceremoniously announced, "We jailed a man for you, John. Wisdom, the gent that come in yesterday."

It took Cromer a long moment to bridle his surprise and ask, "What's he done?"

"Looks like he killed Myrick."

"And it looks like he had reason to," Durwent put in.

Then, reading the mounting bewilderment on the law man's face, he went on to tell of what had happened at the *Fine And Dandy*, and afterward in the hotel room.

By the time Durwent finished, Cromer found the voice to say, "One of you would be doin' me a big favor if you'd take the rig that's out front, along with what's in it, down to Leatherwood's house. He might as well fill out two certificates tonight as one."

Their glances sharpened, and Heffran was quick to ask, "Two? You mean somebody besides Ray? Who?"

"Jesse Ober. Ira found him near the road up toward your place, George. Whoever got him was playin' for keeps. There are three holes in him, any one of which would have done the job."

Walt Heffran said soberly, "There's a soul that won't rest in peace. Any ideas on who he ran into?"

"Not one," Cromer breathed impotently. "Not even the beginning of one."

They had more questions, all of which Cromer answered patiently, briefly. Finally, noticing the jail keys lying on his desk, he went over to pick them up, saying, "George, stick around while I go see Wisdom. We've got some things to talk over about tomorrow."

He thought he saw a look of disappointment come to George Durwent's eyes just then. And a moment later he was puzzled by the man saying, "Wouldn't take me ten minutes to drive Ober down to Leatherwood's, John."

Then Elder offered, "Walt and I can do it." And when Durwent only shrugged, the law man decided his imagination had tricked him in making him think that for some strange reason Durwent was anxious to be away from here.

Longbow's jail was at the back end of the halllway, a single cell walled with granite. The room was pitch black as Cromer entered. And it was cold. Just before he struck a match, the lawman said in strong disgust, "They could've at least built you a fire," and Wisdom's drawl spoke in answer out of the cell's blackness, "Plenty of blankets."

In the flare of the match, Cromer glanced in past the bars to see his prisoner sitting on the low cot, a blanket about his shoulders. Saying nothing, the sheriff lit the lantern hanging by the door and at once stepped across to the wood box alongside a hogsback stove that sat against the grating at the end of the narrow aisle fronting the cell.

He was feeling oddly ill at ease as he began laying wood in the stove, his back to the cell. And as the seconds passed, with no further word from Wisdom, an irritation gathered in him. Finally, after he had whittled the end of a length of pitch pine with his knife, he was crowded into saying, "Let's have the straight of this. All of it."

"What did they tell you?"

"That Myrick was drunk. That he went in at you with an iron in his hand and shut the door. That you must've grabbed the iron and put the hole through him."

He waited for Wisdom to say something, lighting the pine shavings and putting the lid on the stove as they caught. Then, turning to face the cell, he stated sharply, "You're locked up, man! For murder! Is sittin' there playin' dumb all you can think of to do?"

The folds of the blanket at Wisdom's shoulders rose, fell. His blue eyes gave the law man a stare that was steady, utterly solemn. "What else is there to do, sheriff?"

"Talk! Tell me what happened. Exactly."

"You wouldn't believe it."

"You let me decide on that." The stove was beginning to roar softly as Cromer reached out to grip the bars. "You handled Myrick easy enough yesterday when he was sober. What was there to keep you from handlin' him even easier tonight? A drunk's a cinch to knock out, even a big one. Instead, you kill him. Why, man? Why?"

He met Wisdom's speculative glance without letting his own waver. Then Wisdom was saying quietly, "I didn't kill him."

Cromer waved a hand in an angry gesture. "Look, my friend. I'm not askin' for any trumped up story. All I want to know is how it happened. If it was accident, self defense, a jury'll let you off. They might even turn you loose at the inquest. We know Myrick was in the wrong up till the time he closed that door. If you can prove you had to——"

"But I didn't kill him, Cromer," Wisdom broke in. "The shot came through the window. My guess is he was after me, whoever he was. That sounds . . ."

Catching the disbelieving look, the scornful smile that came to the sheriff's face, Wisdom shrugged once more, drawling, "Didn't I say you wouldn't believe it?"

"And I damn' well don't!" Cromer was thinking wearily just then, *I've been wrong about him. If he's out of Yuma and they want him back they can have him*. In a way it was a relief to have made up his mind about this man. What Wisdom had done for Martha no longer counted.

Cromer reached over now and pushed the filled wood box in against the bars, nodding down to it, saying tonelessly, "Help yourself to all the heat you want. One of those sticks'll have to do for liftin' the lid because a man we had in here last winter jammed the lock with the lifter tryin' to break out. And if you get any ideas on burnin' your way out, don't try 'em!" he added caustically. "You'd only wind up dead and smoke up the place. It won't burn."

He was contrarily hoping Wisdom would stop him as he turned the lantern down and opened the hallway door. But no word came from the man as the door closed.

That next morning held more surprises for John Cromer than any had held so far in his lifetime. And only one of these, the weather, was in any degree pleasant.

By nine o'clock, when Brush's yard was filling with rigs and saddle horses, nothing remained of the clouds but a few ragged wisps hanging in the highest canyons. It was sunny, the air bracing but holding a touch of friendly autumn warmth. Yesterday's storm had whitened the peaks and frosted the last trace of delicate green from the patches of quaking asp, leaving them golden, contrasting strongly with the rich emeralds of pine and spruce, and the tawny-red splotches of the oak thickets. It was as though the weather, along with upward of a hundred of his friends, was outdoing itself in paying Matt Ladd fitting tribute.

The first unpleasant surprise came for Cromer when Doc Leatherwood led him aside from a solemn group in the yard and handed him three small, folded pieces of paper, saying worriedly, "These came out of Jesse Ober's pockets, John. Don't know what to make of 'em, but I'll keep my lip buttoned."

Those bills of sale signed by Durwent were only the beginning. Half an hour later Cromer was called into the house to see Ann, to have her tell him that she wanted him to be beside her at the burying. When he reminded her that perhaps it was Durwent's place, not his, she told him bluntly, "John, I'm not marrying George. Don't ask me why just now. But I'm not."

"But how . . ." For the moment speechless, he shortly burst out, "Good Lord! Have you told him?"

"No. And I'm not going to just yet. I'd like you to go see him now. Tell him it was dad's wish that just you and I and the minister be at the grave. You because you were dad's oldest friend."

"But I wasn't! There are any number of—"

"Tell him that anyway."

He somehow managed the chore of carrying that word to Durwent without rousing any suspicion in the man. He had an hour's respite then, until at eleven he brought the surrey and the team of blacks to the foot of the porch steps to take Ann to the graveyard at the top of the knoll behind the house.

They had barely left the yard, with wagons and buggies and people afoot trailing them, before Ann was saying, "John, we've only another minute or two alone. Tell me about Wisdom."

He looked quickly around at her, gruffly asking, "What does it matter about him at a time like this?"

"It matters a great deal. I don't know just why it should, but it does."

Her hushed, utterly serious words jolted him so hard that when he next spoke it was to ask almost gently, "What's got into you this mornin', kid? That about George. Now this about Wisdom. You hardly know the man. He's not worth stewin' over."

"Did he really kill Myrick?"

Seeing how strictly she had ignored his protest, he answered testily. "He did. No doubt about it."

"I can't believe it."

"Believe anything you want."

That tension lay between them until they were coming up on the cedar picketed plot of ground under the widespread branches of a huge greybark growing at the crest of the rise. Then all at once Ann put her hand on his arm saying quietly, "Poor John. You can't understand any of this and I can't explain it. But please have a little faith in me."

"You try a man at times, Ann."

"I know. But just now let's forget that."

The ceremony was as Matt Ladd would have had it, simple, brief, even the preacher refraining from his customary lengthy harangue as though sensing that the people crowded beyond the fence all knew what a good man was going to his grave without having to be told.

It had been decided this morning that Ann would go on in to Longbow to spend the next few days with Martha. Cromer saw them off in the surrey right after the burying, and then spent the time until noon saying his goodbyes as the crowd slowly broke up and took to the road. He was in town by one o'clock, ate a meal and then went straight to his office. It so happened that his first glance toward his desk brought another surprise.

A pale yellow envelope lay on the desk. He sensed with a strong feeling of guilt that it must be an answer to the telegram he had sent day before yesterday, and he picked it up reluctantly, staring down at it fully half a minute before he tore open the envelope and read:—

> CROMER, SHERIFF
> LONGBOW, MONTANA TERR.
>   PRISONER LOCKHART ESCAPED YUMA LATE JULY.
>   WHEREABOUTS UNKNOWN. WARDEN.

For better than an hour now, Rush Wisdom had been standing at the cell's open window, elbows resting on the wide rock sill as he stared through the bars and out across the alley, his thoughts just idling.

Most of the occasional saddle animals and wagons that came along the muddy lane were on their way to or from a blacksmith's barn obliquely opposite. The ring of the anvil across there had begun before seven this morning. Since that hour, Wisdom had from time to time watched the smithy going about his work. Just now he was seeing him using a chain block and tackle hanging from the door's lintel beam to hoist the bed of a wagon up off its rear axle.

There was a strong envy in him over the blacksmith's hearty manner. Most of the time the man was either whistling a tune or joshing his customers in a way that brought Wisdom a deep longing for those carefree days when he'd worked cattle, with no burden on his mind beyond ones like keeping his drift fences tight, hunting down the loafer or mountain cat preying on his herd, fighting the blizzards, or now and then riding to town of a night to raise mild hell with his friends.

Last night, lying here on the cot in the dark, he had felt

a strong bitterness over the irony of being jailed a second time for a second killing he'd had no hand in. But today that bitterness was gone. He was just as convinced as he had been yesterday that George Durwent was the man he had come all this way to hunt down. And he was also just as convinced that he would never go after Durwent until Ann had lost her good opinion of the man.

He wasn't particularly worried about being in here. Cromer had as good as told him outright that no jury was going to convict him for what had happened last night, regardless of whether or not he could make them believe he hadn't fired the bullet that ended Myrick's life. And yesterday's storm had washed out all likelihood of his ever being connected in any way with what had happened to Jesse Ober, even if the man's body was found. So all he had to do was wait.

Just now he heard someone coming along the hallway from the front of the building, and as the lock on the jail door rattled for the third time that day he faced lazily around to see who it might be. The heavy door swung open and John Cromer stepped into the corridor ahead of the cell.

"Plenty to eat this noon?"

"Plenty," Wisdom answered, wondering at the man's almost amiable tone.

Cromer glanced at the filled wood box alongside the stove. "Who brought you the wood?"

"Same man that brought the food. Walt, is he?"

The sheriff nodded. "Walt Heffran."

Putting a shoulder against the cell grating, Cromer drew a knife from pocket, then a pipe, and began working the blade of the knife around the inside of the pipe's bowl. Shortly, without looking at Wisdom, he was saying, "Big turnout for the buryin'. Folks there from all the way to Timberline. Word gets around fast."

"Ladd must've been well liked. How did Ann take it?"

"Like a soldier." The law man's glance all at once lifted, all the pleasantness gone out of it. "So it's 'Ann', eh? Like you know her real well."

Wondering at the change in the man, knowing instantly he'd made a mistake in speaking of Ann so familiarly, Wisdom tried to make the best of it by saying neutrally, "I was out there lookin' for work day before yesterday. Talked to her."

"About what in particular?"

The pointed question made it obvious that the sheriff hadn't just dropped in here for want of something better to do. Perhaps he knew something. He was certainly after information. And now Wisdom had a choice to make, that of telling the man little or nothing, or of leading him on, trying to discover what if anything it was he knew or suspected.

Wisdom's choice was the latter, and he deliberately answered, "We had quite a set to. While we were havin' it, she combed me over for callin' her 'miss'."

"A set to about what?" Cromer was quick to ask.

"Seems I disagreed with what your coroner decided about the way that man Black cashed in. She stuck up for him. And for you."

Cromer's expression took on a strong curiosity. "What about the way Black died?" The click of the knife-blade accented the sharpness of his words.

"I'd told her it looked to me like he hadn't drowned." Keeping his tone casual, Wisdom went on to tell of what he had seen at the river two days ago, noticing the gradual change in the law man's look from one of incredulity to bewildered conviction.

When Wisdom had finished, Cromer let a brief silence run on before saying in heavy sarcasm, "So it just happened you saw all that! Just while passin' by, was it?"

Unable to see what lay behind the other's strange reaction, Wisdom was regretting even the mention of Idaho as he tried to answer off-handedly. "Things sometimes happen like that."

"And sometimes they don't! Wisdom, I don't for one damned minute believe a word of—"

"John!"

Cromer looked around as that call from the hallway cut across his words. The voice was Ann's, and as the sheriff stepped over to glance out the door and answer testily, "Back here!" Wisdom's first eagerness over the prospect of seeing the girl again was dying before a worry as to what might happen if Cromer included her in this talk of Idaho.

"John, old Fred's done an awful thing!" ... Her voice came from close beyond the door ... "He's stolen some letters. Martha's beside herself."

She came on in past Cromer the next moment, stopping short at sight of Wisdom. Then all the wariness and rancour the law man's salty words had left in Wisdom were forgotten as he took in her loveliness. This was the first time he had seen her dressed in anything but a man's outfit. A black, tight-waisted coat accented her tallness and slenderness. The white collar of her dress, showing above the coat, gave her face a quality of delicacy stronger than any he had ever before noticed. She was utterly feminine, utterly desirable.

The look of deep hurt that came to her eyes now at seeing him standing alone in the cell filled Wisdom with an unexpected and awed awareness. It suddenly struck him that the girl had come to mean more to him than anyone ever had. Perhaps she meant even more than his stubborn loyalty to Frank's memory. Then, intruding on this solemn realization, came her hushed words:—

"Rush, did you kill Myrick?"

"No."

He said no more, somehow knowing that nothing but that outright denial was necessary. And as he saw her eyes brighten in gladness and relief, Cromer was inserting dryly, "Let's not get started on that! Now what's this about Fred, kid?"

For several seconds Ann seemed aware of the law man having spoken. Her expression changed subtly as her glance clung to Wisdom's, taking on a radiant wonder as though she was discovering the same thing he had some moments ago.

Finally, with a slight start, she looked at Cromer. "What, John? ... Oh, yes. The two Parker boys were waiting at the house when Martha and I got there. Wanting that headstone Fred's been working on. He was out somewhere, but Martha let them take the stone anyway. They found those letters hidden under it, along with a plug of tobacco. One letter was badly torn."

Cromer shook his head, sighing in disgust. Noticing Wisdom's puzzled look, Ann told him, "None of this can mean much to you, Rush. Remember the girl on the stage the other night, Martha Burke? Her father is ... isn't quite right. He takes things, steals them without really meaning anything by it. Just for the fun of not being caught, I suppose. Anyway, this letter that was nearly ruined was one George had written to someone in his family. John, does George have a brother?"

"None I know of."

"He's never mentioned any of his family to me." The quality of intentness in the stare she was giving Wisdom made it quite plain that she wanted him to listen carefully to what was being said. Then she was adding with a pointed deliberateness, "But whoever Alfred Durwent may be, he lives in Philadelphia. His address is 'Railways Limited'."

"Limited? What would that mean?"

Neither Wisdom nor Ann paid Cromer's question more than a passing attention as Wisdom was jolted by the significance of her remark. He could tell by Ann's mutely questioning look that she at once realized his awareness of what this might mean. Then Cromer was asking, "What's Mart done with the letters?"

"Mailed them. She put George's in a new envelope. Now she's worried over what he may think when she tells him about it."

"What would he think?"

"She's afraid he'll wonder if she read the letter."

"Let him wonder!" Cromer snorted. "Besides, what would it matter if she had?"

"It might matter, John." Ann spoke quietly. And now she looked at Wisdom to ask quietly, "Rush, isn't it time we were telling John what we know?"

Before Wisdom could recover from his surprise, the sheriff was asking irritably, "What's this between you two? About George. This mornin' you said you were through with him, wouldn't marry the man. Now you talk riddles about him to Wisdom here!"

Something Cromer had said roused a hard lift of excitement in Wisdom. "What's that he's saying, Ann?"

"About my not marrying George?" She nodded, "I'm not, Rush." She paused, as though sensing what a difference this would make to him. Then: "Now can we tell John?"

Wisdom was as confused by the question as he had been on hearing of her change of mind toward Durwent. This was all important to him, he wanted to be very sure she knew what she was doing. And now he looked at Cromer. "Sheriff, could we have two minutes by ourselves, Ann and I?"

"What for?" Cromer's suspicious glance shuttled to Ann.

"I'd like to talk to him, John."

Cromer breathed a gusty sigh of bafflement. "Damned if I get any of this!" All at once his glance narrowed, taking on a secretive look. "Come to think of it, there's something in the office we may be needin'. I'll go get it." And he turned out the door, closing it behind him.

A quality of shyness came to Ann's look now. Yet before

Wisdom could speak, she was saying, "I know you're wondering about a lot of things, Rush. But first, did you know they'd found Ober?"

"No." That single word was spoken tonelessly, without excitement.

She nodded. "So far John doesn't know what to make of it. I don't think you need worry."

"I'll take my chances on that, Ann. But this about Durwent. You've got to be—"

"Let me get it said first," she interrupted gently, afterward pausing in a way that let him see how awkward this moment was for her, how difficult it was going to be for her to voice thoughts that had been so personal.

Then, gravely, she was telling him, "Yesterday after you'd gone I did some thinking, Rush. About things I'd never before quite let myself think out. How I've been fighting dad, my friends, almost everyone I know, trying to make them like George. It was while I was trying to see their reasons for not liking him that it struck me how hard he is to know, how little even I know him. He's never talked about home or family for one thing. This Alfred Durwent must be a close relative, yet George has never mentioned him."

"He could've broken off with his folks," Wisdom inserted doggedly. "Plenty of good men do."

"Rush, you can't argue me out of this," she quietly insisted. "I know you're trying to be fair and you have my thanks for that. But the time for overlooking these things about George is past. I hadn't quite realized that until this noon, when Ira, that black man of George's, stopped Martha and me on our way in to town to apologize for not having been at the funeral. I'd missed Ira, expected him to be there, for he thought the world of dad. He was badly broken up about it and wanted me to know it wasn't his fault he hadn't been to see me. I finally pried it out of him that George had told him he had no right to mix with white people and their affairs."

She paused, her eyes taking on the brightness of real anger then as she asked, "How can I respect George when he's that narrow, that mean? When he goes out of his way to hurt someone like Ira simply because of his color? If I had ten friends as good and as loyal as Ira, I'd . . ."

At a loss for words, she hesitated now. Then, in a lower

voice, she stated, "If the reasons I've given so far seem pretty thin; there's still the one you and I found yesterday. George's dealing with Ober. And there's another."

As Wisdom frowned, trying to anticipate what she was to say next, she told him, "Neither you nor dad were quite fair with me yesterday. I think I see now why you weren't. You didn't want to hurt me."

Warily, Wisdom asked, "Hurt you how?"

She smiled faintly. "You're still trying to save my feelings. Why didn't you come straight out yesterday and tell me that George is the one your hunch told you had done Ober's thinking for him?"

"But I—"

"Wait, Rush. Let me finish. You were asking yesterday why the railroad had sent Lockhart in here. I think I know now. He was looking for coal. Something you can't have heard about is that George has been acting queerly about some land dad wanted to give us. George turned down some fine graze and instead insisted on—"

"Your father told me about it," Wisdom cut in soberly. "He happened to mention the coal that afternoon I talked to him."

"He did?" Surprise was as strong in her as it had been in him a minute ago. "Then you've thought of it?"

At Wisdom's slow nod, she asked in an awed way, "Then now can you wonder at my deciding the way I have? When it's possible George has killed to get his hands on that coal? When three men may have died so far because of it?"

"Four, Ann." He saw her stiffen in startlement, and added gravely. "You can count Myrick in on that. Only he wasn't meant to wind up where he did. It looks like the bullet that got him was meant for me."

Incredulity, then a strong revulsion widened her glance. "George?" she breathed in a hushed voice.

"That would be my guess."

There was a finality to Wisdom's words. He no longer had any doubts, any misgivings about causing this girl unhappiness. She had thought this thing through completely on her own, had reached her decision on Durwent without being swayed by anyone. He was free to act now, and he knew what remained to be done as soon as he was out of this jail.

But that thought of Ann having released him to settle the debt for Frank brought on another. With it came that too-

familiar sense of frustration and depression as he realized
that sooner or later he would be leaving this country still a
wanted man.

And now he told her wearily, "You're wrong about one
thing. We can't go to Cromer with any of this. He couldn't
believe it. He'd need ..."

Hesitating, he was all at once remembering that Ann
didn't know who he was, who Frank Lockhart had been. And,
on the point of telling her, he checked himself by realizing
what his explaining would involve. He would have to admit
breaking out of Yuma, would have to tell her of Idaho having
helped him. He had already tried her belief and imagination
beyond any reasonable limit. And now to try it even further
was asking too much of her credulity, of her strange trust in
him.

Besides, he thought, it couldn't matter to her who he
really was. He was important to her only because he had been
a means for exposing Durwent. She was naturally grateful to
him for that, but for that only.

So, instead of saying what he had started to, he told her,
"Maybe one day you'll know the rest, Ann. Something that'll
show you why I have to see this thing finished without going
to Cromer. But I can't explain now."

"The rest?" There was a strong bewilderment in her. "Is
there more?"

That moment the jail door swung open on John Cromer.
He came in eyeing the two of them sternly, his expression
uncompromising as he stepped over and thrust a yellow envelope between the bars, offering it to Wisdom. "Better have
a look at this before you waste any talk."

Wisdom drew the telegram from the envelope and read it.
He could feel his pulse slowing, the color mounting to his face
at the realization of what this meant to him. And a sickening
sense of having failed utterly settled through him as he
glanced bleakly at Cromer, then at Ann.

He held out the telegram to her, saying as she took it,
"Here's the rest, Ann. What I said you might know some
day."

Her puzzled, alarmed glance dropped to the sheet of paper.
Shortly, she was looking at him again, her eyes beseeching
for understanding. "What does it mean?"

"It means he's where he ought to be. Locked up," Cromer
put in with a tone of finality. When he saw that she hadn't

grasped his meaning, he went on, "Remember our talk the other day about Idaho? About this man Lockhart? Something I left out about the letter Lockhart showed me is that it said he was travellin' under a fake handle. For business reasons. His real name was Frank Wisdom."

As Ann caught her breath, her face paling, the sheriff added flatly, "So I've caught myself a killer, Lockhart's killer. His brother."

"No!" Ann cried softly. "No, John!" She was staring disbelievingly at Wisdom. "Rush, is this true?"

"It is, Ann. As far as it goes."

He saw her wince as the words struck her. But then a defiance touched her glance, and she turned on Cromer to say, "Let Rush tell you how it really was! About Jesse Ober. And about George!" Her eyes swung around to Wisdom once more, and a calmness came over her as she asked gently, "Why didn't you tell me, Rush? All this means so much more, knowing who you are."

"Mind lettin' me in on this?" Cromer asked gruffly, dryly. "What about Ober? And Durwent?"

"Rush can tell you how they tricked him, how Ober . . ." Ann's words broke off. Then, her eyes giving Wisdom a look of pleading, she said, "Now you'll have to tell him."

"Looks like I will," Wisdom said resignedly. Then he started talking to Cromer, speaking rapidly, thinking only of getting everything said, everything. He purposely left out any mention of Ober being the man who had testified against him at Laramie, glancing at Ann in a way that warned her not to interrupt.

It was as he was briefly and casually mentioning the months in Yuma that Cromer cut in with a sober comment, "A chunk o' hell, accordin' to what they say. How the devil could you bust out of the place?"

The moment Wisdom answered that, mentioning Idaho, Cromer's interest sharpened. Then shortly Wisdom was telling of meeting Ober here in Lodgepole, of recognizing him. And once again the sheriff interrupted, this time with an involuntary low oath and the hurried admonition, "Go on! What did the sidewinder do?"

The law man's expression took on a quality of grim satisfaction as he listened to the story of the shoot-out with Ober, of Ann having been there and of the long hours it had taken Wisdom to hide the body and start his getaway. Then, as

Wisdom paused to choose his next words, Cromer wanted to know, "Why in the name o' God didn't you keep straight on away from here?"

"Because of me." Ann's words surprised both men. Then she was adding, "Rush would be gone and safe by now but for me."

"That's not quite—"

"And I'll tell you why, John." Ann shook her head as she broke in on Wisdom, her look holding as much meaning for him as her words, "This is my right, Rush. Let me tell it."

She went on then to say how she had tracked Wisdom in the dawn hour of yesterday, to tell of his sign so strangely having joined Ober's. She told of meeting Wisdom at Durwent's place. She had a far greater insight to Wisdom's thoughts than he'd realized; for when it came to the mention of what she suspected of Durwent, she said, "Rush has been sure of all this since yesterday. Dad must have guessed some of it. If it hadn't been for their both wanting to save my feelings, Rush could have gone straight to Durwent and had it out with him."

All of Cromer's truculence, even some of his sureness, had deserted him now. He seemed overwhelmed by what he had heard. "Let's have the rest of it," he said quietly, and listened with an inscrutable set of countenance as Ann continued.

Finally, she was saying despairingly, "So now it's up to you, John."

"So it is." The law man's tone was tinged with a real regret. "But first, here's something more. Leatherwood ran across some bills of sale signed by George in Ober's pockets last night. They were for forty-nine head of cattle. More than George can spare, I'd say. Till just now I'd got to thinkin' maybe it was George who had cashed him in."

Ann seemed strangely unmoved by the news. "It had to be something like that," she said matter-of-factly, in a way that clearly showed how dead in her was any feeling of affection for Durwent. "He was paying Ober for something. He sneaked out so Ira couldn't see him. Because he was doing something to be ashamed of."

"If you could tell me what that something was, kid, we'd be a lot further along."

At the girl's shake of the head, Cromer glanced at Wisdom. "See what this adds up to? Suppose I believe all you say? I'm inclined to, matter of fact. But where does it get me? Nowhere. There's nothin' a man can get his teeth into. No proof of anything."

"Those bills of sale are proof of something, sheriff."

"But of what? On what grounds can I arrest Durwent?"

"You know how he's acted about the coal, John. Dad and you talked that over long ago."

"So we did. But it's proof of nothing. Circumstantial evidence, a court would call it. Durwent would never own up to anything because he's covered his tracks too well. And remember, you're only guessin' on coal bein' the reason Frank Wisdom was sent in here."

"But we know George has written someone in his family connected with a railroad. Get the letter, see what it says, John. It may be the proof you're needing."

"Meddle with the mails?" Cromer shook his head. "They could put me out of office for that. No, I'm hogtied! All I've got to act on is this word from Yuma. I could cut off my hand for ever sendin' the wire that brought it. But here it is. I'm a peace officer sworn to enforce the law."

"You can't send Rush back to prison!"

The sheriff simply lifted his hands outward from sides, let them fall again.

A real fear showed in Ann's eyes then as she breathed, "John, no one knows about this. No one! You could . . ."

"Just turn him loose? You're not thinkin' straight, kid. Remember who made me take this job, who warned me I might have to hurt my friends if I did take it?"

"But Dad would be the first to see the unfairness of this."

"And the first to rear right up out of his grave if I took the law into my own hands."

A weighty silence followed Cromer's deliberate words. Everything had been said that could be said. Each time the law man had countered one of Ann's arguments, or one of his, Wisdom had felt that frustration and helplessness driven deeper in him. And now a stubborn rebellion was rising in him as he fought this growing sense of defeat.

Before he had quite thought out what he would say, he was telling Cromer, "Then don't take the law into your own hands. Keep me locked up here. But give me time."

"Time for what?"

"Maybe I can . . ." At a loss for a definite answer,

Wisdom insisted stubbornly, "Time maybe to get you the proof you're wanting."

"Nothin' but 'maybes', Wisdom," Cromer said heavily.

With a grudging admiration, Wisdom understood then that nothing but hard facts would count with this man, facts that could be proven. Cromer's ironbound sense of justice had been roused over these past few minutes, yet his instinct for wanting to act on what he'd heard was still shackled by his strict sense of duty. Sentiment was strong in the man's makeup, but he wouldn't let sentiment sway him when it came to carrying out that sworn duty.

So now Wisdom gave the only argument that occurred to him. "Look, sheriff. Durwent's bound to give something away if we go at this right. So far as he knows, I'm his only worry. He tried to put me out of the way last night and it didn't come off. He'll—"

"You *think* he did. We're not sure of anything."

"Granted," Wisdom said with a rising irritation. "But if I'm guessin' this right, then as long as I'm around Durwent won't feel safe. Nothing I know of has happened yet to make him think I've tied him in with Ober. But if something was to happen to make him think I might tie him, then he'd have to make a move. Wouldn't he?"

"Something like what?"

Wisdom's thinking, confused until this moment, suddenly ran straight. He answered, "Like your making him think you suspect who I really am."

At the questioning looks both Cromer and Ann gave him, he went on hurriedly, "He'd know you'd never let go once you got your teeth into this thing. So why not tell him you've got a hunch I knew Idaho? Give my being at the inquest as your reason. You'll have to say you've known all along that Idaho was a friend of Frank's, of Lockhart's. And because you think I knew the man, tell Durwent you're getting in touch with Yuma on the slim chance I just might be the brother of Lockhart's they put away."

Cromer's glance narrowed as he considered this. And over the brief silence, Ann said, "Don't you see, John? George would be afraid—"

A hard lift of the law man's hand silenced her. "I see it. But then what?"

"Once there's the chance of your finding out who I really

am, there'd always be the chance you'd uncover the whole story. Durwent would have to do something about me then, wouldn't he?"

The sheriff's eyes shuttled to the cell window. "Something like bustin' that glass out and lettin' you have both barrels of a shotgun?"

Wisdom nodded. "Something like that. But with a blanket hung across the window and the bed moved into the corner, he won't get far with that, will he? And if he does make another try, you'll have your proof."

"So I will," Cromer admitted. "But I don't like it. Not a bit! You'd have to be damn careful."

"I would be," Wisdom told him. Then: "When can you see him?"

"He's coming to town tonight to see me, John," Ann said. "I tried to put him off but he wouldn't listen. I ... I've wondered how I can talk to him without giving away how I feel."

"You can't let him know," Wisdom was quick to say. "Can you keep from it?"

"I'll do anything that'll help you, Rush."

Cromer happened to catch the look on Ann's face as she spoke. It more than surprised him. He was awed by it, and for the first time then he became aware of something as Wisdom was saying, "Sheriff, it might worry Durwent if he knew what happened to his letter, if we're right in thinking it has something to do with this. Martha would have to keep out of his way and not talk to him. How good are you at lyin'? Could you tell him about the letter, let on like you didn't know whether Martha had read it or not?"

The law man thrust aside his speculation over the look Ann had given Wisdom long enough to answer, "If it'll do any good, I'll lie myself blue in the face."

Cromer's strong perplexity over something unlooked-for having entered into this situation stayed with him over the next several minutes, until he and Ann had left the jail and gone along the hallway to his office.

It was as he closed the room's door and leaned back against it that Ann, reading his solemn look, asked, "Is something else wrong, John?"

"This Wisdom," he said gently. "He means a lot to you, doesn't he, kid?"

For an instant her glance wavered, avoiding his in uncertainty and embarrassment. But then her eyes met his again with a look almost of defiance. "He does," she said. "A great deal. So much that I . . ."

"Never mind sayin' it," he told her. "I think I know how it is."

It wasn't until evening, until after dark, that Wisdom saw Cromer again. And then it was only to pass a brief word with him when he brought a big, towel-wrapped plate of food and a mug of coffee in from the restaurant.

"Durwent's here and I missed him," the law man announced glumly after he had set the plate on the wood box so that Wisdom could reach it through the bars. "Saw him goin' down the street while I was on the way out of Walt's with this. He turned in at Burke's, which means Ann must be havin' her troubles."

"Any chance of getting to him later?"

"I'll try, soon as he leaves there. But, friend, we're playin' some mighty long odds."

"They're worth the try."

"We'll see." Cromer was staring at the cell's open window. "Better shut that and hang a blanket, even if he is likely to take the night thinkin' it over." Turning impatiently toward the hallway then, he added, "See you later," and went on out.

That quality of hopelessness in the sheriff's manner drove home a like feeling in Wisdom. And as he sat on the end of the cot, reaching through the bars to eat without much appetite, he was seeing how his emotions had swayed him in his talk with Cromer and Ann this afternoon. That sense of defeat, of desperation, had made him magnify the chances of tricking Durwent into a reckless move. Now he saw clearly that all the man had to do was wait and let matters take their course, even though Cromer was to give him the word they had agreed upon.

He finished eating listlessly, presently building a smoke and reaching through the bars to put more wood into the stove. Only because it was cool in here did he think of the window and go across to close it against the night's chill. Thus reminded of Cromer's parting word, he shoved the cot into the cell's back, outside corner, well out of line with the window.

But then as he picked up a blanket, about to hang it across

the window, he was struck by the absurdity of taking all these precautions, and he tossed the blanket aside. He didn't even bother to turn down the lantern as he stretched out on the cot, closed his eyes and tried to enjoy his smoke.

All that afternoon he had been ignoring an unpleasant thought. It came again now, and wouldn't be thrust aside. Sharply, across his mind's eye, he was seeing the Yuma compound with the blistering sun beating down upon the sandy earth and the red tile roofs. He was hearing the bone dry breeze off the desert rustling the fronds of the palm trees. He was smelling the stink of the Snake Den, feeling the itch and the bite of the mosquitos.

He quickly opened his eyes, unable to stand these memories any longer. And it was then that the thought of breaking out of here came to him.

Until this moment he hadn't considered that possibility, believing they would sooner or later set him free. But now he was struck by the hopelessness of this circumstance, by the irony of being at the mercy of a sheriff who believed him innocent, but who would follow out the letter of the law and in the end ship him back to Yuma. And he sat up and glanced about the cell seeing it in a way he never had before.

His first thought was of the lantern, of the possibility of burning his way out. But the rock walls and Cromer's mention of this very thing last night at once discouraged him. The stove was the next thing to take his eye, and he was thinking for a moment of trying to use its heavy top plate in bending open the bars at the window. But here again came a disappointment as he realized that any part of the stove, built of cast iron, would break before it could bend steel. Then he thought of Ann.

Here was his best chance. Provided he could be persuasive enough, she might be the means of getting him out of here. Everything depended on how strongly she felt about him. Cromer was evidently one of her lifelong friends, and it would take a strong belief in the injustice of what Cromer was doing to make her bring the jail keys, or a hacksaw or crowbar. Considering this, Wisdom ruled out all thought of his feelings toward the girl. They didn't count now. All that mattered was that he should be out of here with the chance of losing himself, of outrunning the threat of a return to Yuma.

A sound from the alley cut across his thoughts this moment. It was one he couldn't define, a muted metallic ringing. He at once put it from mind as his thought clung to Ann. And, as suddenly as he had thought of her as his one chance, he was ruling out that chance in the knowledge that he would never ask her to betray Cromer's trust in her.

A light tapping against the glass at the window less than a minute later brought him bolt upright, swinging his boots to the floor. He rose, putting his back to the wall and quickly reaching up to turn down the lantern and blow it out. His pulse took on a faster beat then as he stared into the darkness in the direction of the window, waiting.

Two seconds later that brittle sound of metal tapping the glass sounded once more, this time loudly. Wisdom eased across until his shoulder was within a foot of the window opening. Then slowly, carefully, he reached out, twisted the window's catch and pulled the sash open.

At once, the harsh whisper of a voice he didn't recognize sounded in to him. "Wisdom, you alone?"

"Yes."

"Here's something for you," came the whisper once more. The next instant there sounded the light clinking of a chain's links against the window's granite ledge. And the voice whispered again, "Take it!"

Wisdom reached out and ran a hand along the broad rock sill. His fingers suddenly touched the cold chain, then a wooden pulley block. He knew at once that this was a block and tackle.

Pulling it in, he crowded back his excitement enough to drawl evenly, "Didn't know I had a friend. Who are you?"

"Never mind! But give me twenty minutes to get clear of town before you use this."

"Why should I use it? They've got nothing on me. They'll turn me loose sooner or later."

"You just think they will! Do you know Cromer thinks you killed Ober and is trying to prove it?"

Wisdom was trying hard to think of some way of making whoever this was speak aloud. And now he asked dryly, "Who's Ober? Never heard of him."

Mocking, low laughter echoed in through the window. "No? You never did?" There was a moment of silence. Then, his whisper roughened by a rising impatience, the man out there asked, "Do you want them to hang you?"

Wisdom waited tensely, not answering, wanting his silence to play on the other's nerves.

Suddenly then, the voice sounded again. But this time it spoke aloud, saying scornfully, "You fool, take your chance or leave it!"

The voice was George Durwent's.

Seven

JOHN CROMER didn't do justice to his elk roast and apple pie supper at Walt Heffran's that evening. He was too nervous, too preoccupied in thinking back on his talk with George Durwent to relish the food.

Their meeting had been the exact opposite of what he had planned. For, while he was walking the street looking for Durwent, the man had unexpectedly hailed him from a doorway opposite.

Durwent had unceremoniously begun the conversation with some scalding comments on Fred Burke's failing, even suggesting that the old man be jailed. It had been easy for Cromer to pretend ignorance of exactly what had happened, of whether or not Martha had read the letter. And, strangely enough, it had been relatively simple for him afterward to sift their talk in a perfectly natural way to Wisdom.

The whole thing had seemed just right to him from the moment of their encounter to Durwent's parting word, "Can't say that I envy you your work, John. But at times it must be interesting. This Lockhart affair, for instance. I'd really like to know how your guess on Wisdom turns out. Let me know, will you?"

Looking back over those two or three minutes, Cromer decided that the reason for their going so smoothly lay in Durwent having been inexplicably nervous, more nervous than he had himself. He supposed that Durwent having seen Ann earlier, learning of what had happened to his letter, was the cause of this. At any rate, he was fairly sure that Durwent had accepted what he said at its face value, without any suspicion that anything was out of line.

Leaving Heffran's, the sheriff changed his mind about going back to the jail and seeing Wisdom. Instead, he went on across the street to Red Ennis's, hoping a game of snooker would take his mind off his troubles, and Wisdom's. He had a guilty conscience and was fighting it, knowing there was nothing to stop him from taking the attitude that Wisdom, able to claim self defense in the shooting of Myrick, should at once be set free. He believed the man's story of Ober, and of Durwent. But he also believed that there were right and wrong ways of doing things. The way he had picked he stubbornly told himself was the right one.

Ordinarily, he was an expert with the cue and could most always have a game on the house, even playing against Ennis. Tonight was a different story. He couldn't seem to find a cue with a tip that would take chalk. After his third try he began complaining to Ennis, a thing he seldom did except in a joking way; and tonight he wasn't joking.

He and Ennis were having some hot words when he felt a tug at his sleeve and looked around to find Doc Leatherwood's youngster, Jim, staring up at him in a worried way. The next moment the boy was saying excitedly. "You better get up there to the jail, sheriff! I was walkin' the alley when the man in there called out to me. Told me to find you quick as I could! You're to—"

"Thanks, Jim," the law interrupted, laying his cue on the table and starting for the door. As an afterthought, he reached into a pocket, found a dime and stopped long enough to toss it to the youngster and at the same time tell Ennis, "Forget the grousin', Red. Guess I'm off my feed tonight."

On his way up the street, that first excitement calmed in him as he told himself there might be any number of reasons for Wisdom wanting to see him. The wood box might be empty, the lantern might have run out of oil. Or Wisdom might have decided to argue this affair again; and Cromer wasn't looking forward to any such argument.

He slammed the courthouse door as he entered and had taken barely three strides along the wide, dark hallway when suddenly a faint, metallic banging sounded from the back of the building, from the jail. Excitement rose in him once more then, and he ran the last few steps to the jail door, his fingers fumbling nervously for the right key.

The cell lantern's weak light showed as the door swung open. Cromer went on in to find his prisoner standing close behind the bars. He saw that Wisdom held something in his hands, but paid it scarcely any attention as he asked, "Why all the racket?"

Wisdom answered by lifting what he was holding. Only then did Cromer really look at it, see the wooden pulleys and the light chain. And as outright astonishment hit him, he breathed, "Where'd you get that?"

"Through the window. Half an hour ago."

Cromer's jaw went slack. "Durwent?"

Wisdom nodded. "Durwent. He asked for twenty minutes to get clear before I broke out. Said he'd talked to you. Said you were tryin' to hang the Ober business on me."

"But we never once mentioned Ober."

Again Wisdom nodded, this time smiling sparely. He waited a long moment, giving Cromer time to take it all in. Then, with a glance at the block and tackle, he asked, "Is this proof enough, sheriff?"

"More than enough," came Cromer's sober answer.

Reaching out then, Wisdom dropped the block and tackle onto the foot of the cell cot. He looked around at Cromer again, then at the lock on the cell door. He didn't say anything. There was no need to say anything.

An angry look hardened the severe lines of Cromer's thin face just then, though he was staring at the cell's blanket-draped window rather than at Wisdom. And shortly he was saying in an awed, tight voice, "Never quite believed it of him till now. Think what it means! His courtin' Ann all this time just for the chance of . . ."

As he paused, having spoken more to himself than to Wisdom, his look became bleak, almost hateful. Wisdom waited for him to continue and, when he didn't, drawled, "We're wastin' time, Cromer. Get your key out."

The sheriff's glance abruptly shifted to Wisdom, softening as he shook his head. "There'll be no key just yet, my friend. This is my play from here on out. I'm the law and I go after him."

An expression first of disbelief, then of blazing anger, gathered on Wisdom's lean face. "Your play! After I've come all this—"

"Mine it is," Cromer broke in quietly. With a glance toward the cot, the law man continued, "That's a pretty light rig for what Durwent meant it to do. It'll take you a lot of time if it works at all." He eased over to the door, looking back to say, "Then there'll be this to bust through. Better just sit tight till I get back, Wisdom."

"Wait!" Wisdom called sharply as the door was swinging shut behind the sheriff. "Take me with you! You're goin' up against two men. One's—" The slam of the heavy door shut out the sound of his rising voice.

John Cromer faintly heard Wisdom shout once more as he went along the hallway to his office. He didn't bother lighting a lamp as he crossed the room to his desk, opened its top drawer and took a .44 Navy Colt's from it. He opened the weapon's loading gate, holding it to the faint light at the street window as he spun the cylinder, checking it, seeing that all but one chamber was loaded.

His feeling was one of solemn satisfaction then as he headed out onto the street and turned up it toward Arnholt's stable, thinking of Durwent. He had never before despised and scorned anyone with quite this intensity. The pattern of Durwent's deception lay perfectly clear before him now, and the errand he was setting out upon seemed rightfully his, as he had told Wisdom. Durwent had always rubbed him the wrong way, the man had never seemed good enough for Ann despite his polished ways and smooth talk. It shocked him to think of what a near thing this had been for Ann, to think of what her life might have been had she married Durwent.

This pressure of the Colt's wedged in his belt gave him an assurance he seldom felt, a positive belief in his physical superiority over most anyone. He was always absolutely sure of himself with a handgun. Because of this he rarely carried one, his reasoning being that either a gun or a badge conferred upon the wearer an advantage that was ordinarily dangerous even for a peace officer to assume. He had never lorded it over any man, and so far this strict humility in him had paid dividends. For everyone he had ever considered his friend in the days before he took office still remained his friend. No one he knew of had ever resented his being sheriff simply because he was as he'd always been.

He was on his way across the intersection above the hotel when he saw old Fred Burke cutting across ahead of him, hurrying. And as he neared the walk, well ahead of the man, Burke called, "Hold up, John! Want to see you."

Cromer stopped, saying impatiently as the other approached "Make it short, Fred. I'm in a hurry."

Burke was out of breath but didn't wait to catch it, at

once beginning, "John, I'm sorry as hell about those letters."
He lifted his hands, staring at them. "When Mart told me
about it I could've cut these off! Think of all the trouble I
made!"

"Isn't the first time, Fred."

"I know. Only, damn it, I've never before quite got what
it meant. John, I'm finished with swipin' things!"

"Sure, Fred. Sure you are," Cromer drawled, adding
hurriedly, "We'll talk it over later. But right now you could
do something for me."

"Anything. Name it."

"Go straight on home. Tell Ann everything's all right with
Wisdom. He's in the clear. Tell her I've gone out to get
Durwent."

"Get George?" The old man was bewildered. "How? What
he—"

"Never mind for now, Fred. You'll know it all soon
enough. Just do as I say. Can I count on you?"

"Why sure. But—"

"Got to be gettin' on," Cromer interrupted. He stepped
onto the walk and started away, saying, "Remember, tell her
she's not to worry about Wisdom."

A blend of exultancy and keen relief gripped Durwent all
the way home, that feeling being of such sustained intensity
that he scarcely noticed the passage of time. He had been
unbelievably lucky, John Cromer had been unbelievably
stupid. By morning Wisdom should be sixty or seventy miles
from Longbow. That knowledge of Cromer suspecting him
of having killed Ober should carry the man far away from
here, and fast.

Durwent hadn't felt quite this good even after watching
Matt Ladd die, for then he'd had the worry of Ober on his
mind. Now he hadn't a worry. There was nothing, absolutely
nothing, any longer standing between him and his ambition.

He began seeing things slightly differently about the time
he left the main road and cut through the timber toward his
layout. First came the disquieting thought that Ann's reserved
manner toward him, which had seemed so natural because of
the past two trying days, might have a deeper meaning than
he'd put to it. Next, he began wondering about John
Cromer's not knowing whether or not Martha had read the

letter. That seemed unnatural when he came to think of it carefully, close as the sheriff was to Fred Burke's old-maidish daughter.

But strangest of all was the law man having confided his suspicions of Wisdom to anyone. Until now that had seemed a freak of circumstance, proof to Durwent that even men of the strictest principles could sometimes be inconsistent.

By the time he had turned the chestnut into the corral and was starting to walk on up to the house, he was really worried. He saw abruptly that his talk with Cromer had thrown him too far off balance, had left him too panicked to see its inconsistency. And the realization of that now jolted him so hard that he halted sharply.

Suddenly startled and afraid, he understood at once that what he had learned from Cromer hadn't been a pure stroke of luck after all. There had instead been something purposeful in Cromer, always close-mouthed, having picked him, someone he didn't particularly like, as one to confide in.

Just as suddenly he was associating this oddity with Ann's strange coolness toward him this morning at the funeral and this evening at the Burkes'. He was now certain of something that had until this moment been a strong possibility, that possibility having prompted his rash decision to help Wisdom break jail so he could be rid of the man once and for all. Martha Burke had read his letter. She had told Ann about it. She had told Cromer.

Starting toward the house once more, he was already considering various ways of explaining the letter should he be asked about it. What he had written he had worded very obscurely. Luckily, he hadn't once used the word "coal", or even a proper name. If the sheriff tried to pin him down to the face of knowing about Lockhart, he could say he had only recently had word from Alfred about the railroad having sent a man into the country. He could claim that Alfred had mentioned no names, had said nothing of why a geologist had been sent to Longbow, had asked him to treat the matter in the strictest confidence. Better yet, if there was time he could write Alfred and ask for such a letter to give Cromer as proof of knowing none of the details.

He was absorbed in this devious thinking as he walked in on the rear of the house and caught sight of Ira moving between the kitchen window and a lamp beyond. Thus reminded of a few uncomfortable moments Ann had given him this evening, a strong anger at once hit him. He thrust aside his worry over the letter, tramped heavily across the stoop to the back door and threw it open so hard that it hit the wall.

He walked on into the room with an angry scowl on his face, glaring at Ira. But the black man turned to the stove without noticing his expression, saying cheerily, "You get on in there and sit down, boss. I'll have you a steak fried up sooner'n you can get settled."

"Ira, why did you stop Ann this morning and tell her what you did?"

The chill in Durwent's tone brought Ira wheeling quickly around, his dark face showing an alarm that was close to fear. "Boss, I only wanted for her to—"

"Boss be damned!" Durwent burst out, pulling off his gloves with a savage gesture as he stepped in on the black man. "You'll speak to me as you were taught to!"

"Y-yes, sir."

Durwent suddenly struck out with the gloves, catching the other hard across the face. And as Ira backed into the stove, the Englishman breathed furiously, "Make a fool of me, will you! Why, I'll take the whip to you, you damned ungrateful nigger! I'll ..."

Ira edged further away, his eyes wide open in a terror-stricken, unbelieving stare. "Please, Mist' George! I was only tryin' to make it up to Miss Ann. She's about my best—"

"Quiet!" His hand drawn back to strike again, Durwent all at once froze motionless, head cocked, listening.

The sound of a trotting horse rode faintly in out of the night from the direction of the meadow. And at once the wrathful look faded from Durwent's eyes before one of alarm. He wheeled toward the door leading to the front of the house, saying sharply, "Blow out that lamp and get the shotgun! Get outside and stay there. If this is trouble, watch out for me! No matter who it is. Understand that? No matter who!"

"You in trouble?" Ira asked. "What—"

"Move, damn you!" Durwent was already on his way along the short hallway to his bedroom.

He wheeled into the room's darkness and across to the bed, knocking the pillow aside and snatching up a pepper-box derringer from the sheet. But then, about to thrust it inside his shirt, he hesitated, undecided. Finally he dropped the weapon onto the bed again and went on out and into the living room, making for the deep easy chair alongside the lamp at the end of the table.

A second after he had eased down into the chair he was again hearing the horse out there, the sound louder now. He caught the gentle closing of the back door and took a quick glance down the hallway, the panic in him quieting a little when he saw that the kitchen was dark.

He took a newspaper from the table, opened it across his lap and stretched out deeper in the chair. He looked at the paper, not seeing the print as he listened to the slow stomp of the horse coming in across the yard.

The next few seconds drew his nerves tighter. He waited until the animal's measured tread had stopped close before the house. Then, lazily, he laid the paper aside and rose from the chair. He took his time about going to the door, about opening it and calling out, "Who's there?"

He got no answer beyond the sound of a man's light tread mounting the porch steps. And in that moment he was almost panicked into wheeling inside and slamming the door in the face of whoever this was. But he stood his ground, seeing an indistinct shape moving in across the porch.

He spoke again. "Who is it?" and this time had an answer, "Just me, George."

It was John Cromer's voice, and at once stark fear struck through Durwent. Somehow, he managed to step back from the door, to say with a lame cordiality, "Come in . . . come in, John. What brings you out so late?"

Cromer stepped into the doorway an instant later. His thin face wore as serious an expression as Durwent had ever seen on it. His eyes fixed Durwent with a steady, unfriendly stare.

"Where's Ira, George?"

"Ira?" Durwent was annoyed at the edge to his voice and tried to control it as he went on, "He should be asleep somewhere up near the north fence. He has a full day tomorrow stapling that wire. But why would you ask?"

"Turn around, George."

Frowning, Durwent was about to say something when Cromer repeated more sharply, "Turn around!"

Hesitantly, Durwent did turn. And a moment later Cromer stepped in behind him, running hands swiftly along the line of his belt, slapping his pockets. Then the law man was saying, "George, I'm arresting you for the murder of Ray Myrick."

Durwent wheeled around with such suddenness that Cromer's hand streaked in under his coat and settled into line very fast, fisting the Navy Colt's. "It wouldn't take much to crowd me into using this," the law man intoned flatly.

Durwent had been taken completely by surprise by the charge the sheriff made. Yet now that aloofness so deeply ingrained in his nature rose to steady him. And shortly he could ask, "Is my hearing failing me? Are you really serious?" with a semblance of calm.

Cromer let the gun drop slowly to his side. "Myrick'll do for a beginnin'. Later we may get around to a couple more."

The faint creaking of a board on the porch made Durwent hurry to cover the sound by asking, "A couple more what, sheriff?"

"Murders."

Cromer was standing with his back to the open door, and Durwent had to shift his glance barely perceptibly to stare beyond the law man and out into the darkness. He caught two feeble lines of reflected lamplight from an object out there and knew it to be Ira's shotgun. And suddenly his shaken nerve steadied until he could ignore the fear of a moment ago.

"And who might the two be?"

Cromer's expression took on a pity just then, almost a sadness, as he answered, "Better not waste your time and mine stallin' it out any longer, George. Wisdom's told it all. About Ober in Laramie, about the coal. A jury can make its own guess on Idaho."

Durwent listened to that indictment placidly, his only emotion one of scorn and dislike for this man. But then a thought came that unsettled him to the point where a real concern edged his tone as he asked, "How much of this does Ann know?"

"All of it. Every bit."

The numbing shock and sense of utter defeat that settled through Durwent then reminded him clearly of a feeling he'd had years ago. Pride and the breadth of an ocean had saved him then, yet pride alone was all he could call on now.

He said loudly, "Shoot this fool if he moves, Ira!"

He saw Cromer's frame go rigid, saw the man's wrist tighten against the weight of the Colt's. And he quickly said, "Let him know you're there, Ira!"

The black man's shape took on form against the outward darkness, and the sound of the step that brought him into the doorway was plainly audible. "I'm here sure enough, boss."

A thin, cold smile settled across Durwent's face. "He has my Greener aimed at your back, John. Better drop your gun."

Cromer stood there rigid a moment, as though ready to wheel and lift the Colt's. But then his fingers opened, the .44 thudding to the floor. Durwent came warily in, knelt beyond the law man's reach and picked up the gun. Then, stepping away from Cromer, he drew back the hammer of the Colt's, saying as he lifted it, "Go on back out there, Ira. We're likely to have another caller in a few minutes. It'll be Wisdom. Bring him on in when he gets here."

Within two minutes after the sound of Cromer's steps had faded along the courthouse hallway, the lantern was out and the block and tackle rigged between the window and the cell's partition.

That first impotent rage in Wisdom at Cromer's having headed out alone after Durwent left him as he realized that the sheriff had acted typically, even generously. He understood the point Cromer had made in having a private score to settle with the Englishman. But he also had his own to settle with the man. It would be a betrayal of Frank's memory simply to wait for Cromer's return. So he was on his way out.

Cromer had obligingly pointed out that the block and tackle was light, that if he did break out the front of the cell he would still have the heavy plank door to force. So he had taken a triangular hitch as low as he could on two of the cell's front bars, chaining the other end to the centre of one of the window's.

After he had taken up the slack between the two pulleys, he put his full strength into the pull for only an instant, feeling the straining of the rig without anything giving. The window bar was short, tough, deeply imbedded in rock. It would take more pull than the block and tackle could give to make it bend or break loose.

He went to the front of the cell near the stove and, groping in the darkness, finally found an arm-length chunk of pine twice as thick as his wrist. Bringing it to the window, he wedged one end of it in between the bar that was chained and its neighbor. Tightening the tackle once more, he lifted a boot, put it against the length of wood. Then, braced doubled-over between the pull on the chain and the thrust of his boot against the levering chunk of pine, he threw all the rawhide strength of his back and leg muscles into straightening his body.

Slack came into the chain so suddenly that he lost his footing and rolled to the floor, a chunk of rock falling from the window's sill hitting him on the point of the shoulder. When he came erect again and felt of the bar it was to find its top end torn out of the rock.

Moving the hitch to the top end of the bar and bending it further inward with the block and tackle took but ten more seconds. Then, pausing to listen for any sound along the alley, hearing none, he put his head between the bars, turned his shoulders sideways and squeezed his way out.

He dropped head-first to the ground below the window, at once rolling violently aside, then coming erect in a lunge for the between-buildings passageway alongside the courthouse. Until he stood with back to the brick wall, breathing shallowly, listening, he wasn't at all sure that Durwent hadn't intended waiting out there for another try at him. But as the seconds ran on without his hearing anything beyond faint noises from the street, he decided that the man's one thought had been to let him break out only so that he could leave the country.

He had a choice to make. He could either start looking for Durwent here in town, or he could play the chance that the man had ridden on out home. It was that quality of furtiveness he supposed must be so strong in Durwent's makeup that made him decide the man could no longer be in town. Durwent had asked for time to get clear before he broke out. The man had evidently been serious about not wanting to be around when the break was made.

Once he'd convinced himself of that, Wisdom hurried on along the passageway to its end. A glance along the street showed him the walk empty as far as he could see in either direction. He stepped out casually then, took to the walk and turned in at the courthouse doorway. Five seconds later he was standing in Cromer's office, his back to the closed door, listening again. A dead quiet lay through the building.

He had hoped there would be a blind at the street window, but there was none. So putting his back to the window, he thumbed a match alight, his glance shuttling quickly over the room. In the instant before he shook the flame out, he saw his hat, shell-belt and Colt's hanging from the head of a rocker across by the fireplace.

Seven minutes later, he was leading the roan out the back gate of Ned Arnholt's corral. Once in the saddle, he put the animal out the alley at a run. The need for caution had passed. Cromer was a good quarter-hour ahead of him.

This night had taken on a quality of outright terror for Ira. He had been trembling, more afraid than ever before in his life as he came onto the porch there at Cromer's back with the shotgun. He hadn't dared let his hand stray anywhere near the Greener's triggers. Nothing but blind devotion had carried him that final step into the doorway when Durwent called to him. And nothing but that same blind devotion had sent him out into the darkness again to wait for whoever it was Durwent had said might be coming.

He didn't know how all this had come about, or why. He did know that sooner or later he would be punished for his part in it. He had always looked up to John Cromer as being a fine man, and to find that Durwent was going against the sheriff, defying the law, struck him as being so sinful that he said a prayer for Durwent on his way out to the near margin of the meadow.

Only when he had hunkered down behind a patch of oak close to the road did he think back and try to remember what Cromer and Durwent had been talking about. He'd been too afraid really to listen. But the word "murder" had stuck in his brain like a tick. And now as he thought of Cromer having used it, the frightening possibility of George Durwent having killed came to him.

He refused to believe that of Durwent, refused to even though he knew how queerly the man had been acting lately. He told himself that whatever it was Durwent had done, he had done unknowingly, maybe without thinking, the same as he had lost his head a few minutes ago there in the kitchen and struck out with his gloves. Something was wrong with Durwent. He was worried, not thinking right. If his thinking had been right, he would never have taken the stand he had about Ira going to Matt Ladd's funeral.

Maybe all this had something to do with Durwent getting mixed up with Jesse Ober. Ira wasn't curious by nature. But he had known that Durwent had several times met someone outside the house at night, and on at least two occasions had recognized the tracks of Ober's big claybank. It had worried him to think of Durwent having anything at all to do with trash like Ober, though he hadn't dared mention it.

But all this didn't count now. Durwent was in real trouble of some kind. He needed help. He needed time to explain whatever was the matter to Cromer. He couldn't really have done anything wrong. It just looked that way. Thinking this, Ira began to feel a little better.

He had been squatting there behind the thicket about ten minutes, the shotgun cradled in his lap, when a sound that might have been the snapping of a branch came from the edge of the meadow, startling him. He sat very still, straining to listen, eyeing the dense shadows along the timber margin. Abruptly a walking horse's slow and muffled hoof whisper reached him. A moment later he caught the faint shadow of a horse and rider drifting slowly toward him along the edge of the pines.

Settling back down and further out of sight, he eased the shotgun around till it was pointing toward the rider. He was suddenly remembering who it was Durwent had said he was expecting. Wisdom. The very thought of the man who had whipped Myrick tuned his senses to a sharper wariness. Had he known of Wisdom's arrest, of Myrick's death, he couldn't have been more alert. He gripped the Greener tighter, watching the rider pause briefly, then start walking the horse this way again. He hooked his thumb over the shotgun's hammers.

But then, in the act of cocking both barrels, he hesitated. He wasn't going to shoot a man, especially a good man. Everything he'd heard in town yesterday about Wisdom had been good. So he wouldn't do him any harm. He'd bring him in to the house as Durwent had asked, but he'd use the shotgun only for show.

It was several more seconds before he saw that Wisdom was swinging to the right and would miss the thicket by a good fifty feet. So he reached down and pulled off his boots, came to a crouch and catfooted down along the line of the thicket. He could hear the horse plainly now, hear the swish of the hooves through the grass. His pulse was pounding like a jack hammer, and he had to keep telling himself that now was no time to be afraid, that Durwent was counting on him.

He reached the end of the thicket, thought about going further and decided against it. Wisdom was close enough now, sixty or seventy feet away, so that the starlight let him see he was a big man, rangy and powerful across the shoulders. For the first time then, it occurred to Ira that the man might make a fight of it. He hoped he wouldn't. To kill was a sin, and he was no sinner.

Wisdom picked this moment to tighten rein and bring the roan to a stand. He could see the house lights plainly through the trees, could even make out a horse standing close below the porch steps. Cromer was evidently inside the house. He was probably talking to Durwent, probably had the handcuffs on the man, which meant that this slow, cautious approach was wasted. Still, Wisdom was thinking, having played this so carefully this far, now was no time to turn careless.

This was as far as he would risk taking the horse. He swung down out of the saddle slowly, and afterward led the roan to the end of a nearby oak thicket. He was leaning over, winding the reins around a branch, when a husky voice close at hand said:—

"Just you stand there, mister! Right still!"

Wisdom instinctively wheeled to the right, facing the voice. He saw Ira crouched there barely twelve feet away. He saw the shotgun. And the outspread fingers of his right hand, clawed for the draw, relaxed.

Ira came slowly erect, saying hoarsely, "Lift your hands! Be still now!"

For perhaps three seconds Wisdom didn't move, a hot blaze of outrage and disappointment almost driving him to lunge sideways and try to draw the Colt's before Ira could pull trigger. But then he was remembering Matt Ladd's judgment of this black man. And, very carefully he lifted hands to the level of his shoulders.

Ira moved on around him, came in behind him so soundlessly that the sudden pressure of the Greener's barrels against his spine brought surprise. His coat was pulled aside and, before he could think of moving, the weight of the Colt's had left his belt. Then the shotgun was pushing him forward, and Ira was saying, "Go on in, mister. And don't try nothin'! This buckshot's no thing to fool around with."

A grim resignation was settling through Wisdom as he slowly paced along the thicket's edge. He knew without Ira telling him that John Cromer was in trouble, maybe dead. It was this thought that made him drawl, "So Durwent's killed another man?"

"Another? What you mean? Mist' George's killed nobody! Don't you try and say he has!"

There was a tightness and strong anger in Ira's tone, along with a disbelief that was unmistakable. And suddenly Wisdom understood something that put more meaning to what Ann had said of the man this afternoon. A faint excitement rose in him then that made him say deliberately, "Ira, I'm going to stop right here. We're going to talk. Keep that gun on me if you want, but there are some things I have to tell you."

"You keep right on!" Ira said hurriedly. "Do your talkin' to the boss."

Wisdom's back muscles tightened as he ignored the man's word and halted abruptly, turning around. Ira had stopped. He backed away a step now, lifting the Greener to shoulder. "You go on or I blow a hole through you! Swear I will!"

"You won't," Wisdom said levelly. "You're too good a man to kill another, Ira. Matt Ladd's told me about you. So has Ann. She and I talked about you only this afternoon."

The shotgun's barrels wavered, dropped. And it was in a frightened, low voice that Ira said, "You're lyin'! You never did talk to Miss Ann 'bout me. You're here to make trouble and I'm takin' you in!"

"Ann told me how you stopped her along the road today. Told me how sorry you were you didn't get to see Matt buried."

The black man stood there too confused to speak. And Wisdom went on, "You can't know what Durwent's done or you wouldn't be here now, Ira. He's a murderer."

"You're lyin' again!" Ira burst out, his voice rising to a near shout.

"What did the sheriff say, Ira?" Wisdom waited out a three second interval before insisting, "What did he say when he came in to arrest Durwent? What have you done with him?"

Ira jerked the Greener viciously in line once more. "You keep on walkin' now! No more talk like that!"

Reading the panic in the other's voice, Wisdom slowly moved his head from side to side. "Not yet. Before you take me in there, you're going to understand something. Ann isn't marrying Durwent."

"That's nothin' to do with me!"

"It's got a lot to do with you, Ira. You like Ann, don't you?"

" 'Course I do. But you quit—"

"Wait, Ira! Listen," Wisdom interrupted sharply, a ring of angry authority in his voice. "The reason Ann isn't marrying Durwent is that he's been doing something behind her back. He and Ober."

"Ober? What about him?"

The quality of rising alarm in the black man's voice made Wisdom very careful as he chose his next words. "Together they've killed three men, Ira. Black to begin with. Remember him? And Myrick. Then another you don't know."

"Myrick? He's dead?"

"He is. If you'd been at the funeral today, you'd have heard about it. I can't tell you the rest now, but they were trying to steal from Ann. She only just found out about—"

"Ira!" A shout from the house cut across Wisdom's words. "Who's out there?"

Knowing instantly that the voice was Durwent's, Wisdom said, "Cromer'll never live till morning if you answer, Ira!"

He was standing close enough to the black man to see him hesitate, to hear him draw in his breath to shout. And that moment he lunged.

Ira screamed, "Boss, watch out!" and drove his stocky shape hard to the side. He lined the shotgun at Wisdom. But then, in sudden indecision, he lifted it higher and swung it club fashion. Wisdom took the numbing impact of the heavy barrels against a shoulder a split-second before his fist caught Ira full against the temple.

The Negro whimpered in pain as he went to his knees. He sobbed helplessly as the Greener was wrenched from his grip. The frantic reach he made to hip pocket for Wisdom's Colt's was a full second too late. For as he drew the weapon Wisdom hit him full on the jaw and he slumped face down onto the grass.

Wisdom snatched the Colt's from the man's loose grip, turned and started running toward the house lights. He had taken barely two strides when the lampglow in the two windows faded, then died out altogether. He ran faster, leaving the line of the road now and cutting through the trees, the outline of the house quite plain in the starlight as he closed on it.

He was within a hundred feet of the porch, running his hardest, when a gunshot's rosy wink of light exploded at him from the house's far corner. He let his knees buckle and fell in a headlong, rolling dive. He lay there looking across the barrel of the Colt's as an indistinct shadow moved out from the house corner. And instantly the thunder clap of another shot came at him.

He felt rather than heard the bullet strike very close to his right. Then, with deliberate care, he squeezed the trigger of the Colt's.

The shadow that was George Durwent jerked toward the shelter of the wall corner. Wisdom threw another shot at it, and another. He saw Durwent wheel around and stagger away from the house. Then suddenly the man's shape was slowly settling into the obscurity of the ground.

It was after midnight when John Cromer and Wisdom came down along Longbow's main street, their horses at a walk. Neither had spoken throughout this long ride. In fact, not a word had passed between them since they had left Ira sobbing there in the dark, kneeling alongside Durwent's body.

They were approaching the hump-roofed shape of Arnholt's barn when Wisdom finally broke that long silence by asking, "What time does the stage go north tomorrow, John?"

"Little after nine," came Cromer's answer. Then abruptly he was asking, "Is that light comin' from my hangout?"

Wisdom stared sleepily along past the lighted lobby windows of the hotel to the courthouse. One window there showed a light. "Looks like it."

"Hell," Cromer breathed, "Now what?" Then, because it suddenly came to him what the light must mean, he drawled, "Better stick with me till we see what's gone wrong."

Wisdom glanced at him, shrugged, said, "Anything you say," and they went on, passing Arnholt's, then the street crossing and the hotel.

As they slanted across to the courthouse tie rail, Cromer said, "Don't bother gettin' down. This won't take but a minute." He came tiredly aground, tossed reins over the pole and went on into the building.

He was unsurprised when he entered the office to find Ann standing watching the door. He had barely closed it when she was asking, "Where is he?"

"Dead," Cromer said.

He saw the color go from her face, saw the sudden dread and fear in her eyes. And he was quick to say, "George, not Wisdom, kid. Rush is right out front waitin' for me." He smiled broadly then, adding, "Or for you."

It did him good to see the look on her face then, the shyness that came to it, the delight. The next moment she was covering her confusion by saying, "Tell me about it, John."

Cromer sighed heavily. "There's a man to take along, that Wisdom. Got me out of a real tight fix. I'd bulled my way straight on in to George's place and had the luck to get Ira behind me with a gun. Afterward, George had me roped in a chair. Then Wisdom showed up. It was over before you could bat an eye."

"Did George admit anything?"

"He did." The law man shook his head in a wondering way. "Never saw anything like the way he talked. Proud of what he'd done. Proud of how far ahead he planned to get rid of Frank Wisdom. He did that himself. It was Ober settled for Idaho. George had me scared purple. Came right out and said they'd find me and Wisdom lyin' up somewhere along the pass. He was going to head out and take Ira with him."

"Is Ira all right?"

"He will be. Right now he's busted up bad. Wouldn't come in with us. Wanted to dig the grave tonight."

"He must know he'll have a home with me." Ann was silent a long moment before asking, "And Rush, John?"

Cromer shrugged. "He asked about the northbound in the mornin'."

"He's leaving, then? He wants to leave?"

The hurt that was in Ann's eyes made Cromer say gently, "No one's invited him to stay, kid."

He saw that his words had surprised her. The next moment

she abruptly came on past him to the door. And as she opened it, Cromer drawled, "Luck."

His word made her look around. Gravely, she told him, "You deserve some of your own. John, try asking Martha."

"I have."

"Try again. We had a talk tonight. This time it might turn out differently."

Wisdom had built a cigarette, and as he sat there smoking it he was trying for the first time to look ahead, wondering what it would be like to be leaving here tomorrow, to be heading home. He had always looked forward to a feeling of rightness, of peace, once the accounting for Frank had been settled. Instead there was a nagging restlessness in him, an indefinable regret. He wasn't looking forward to much of anything, when he came to think of it. The wild hills behind Cimarron no longer beckoned as they had at Yuma, or as they had even three days ago here in Longbow. It was almost as though he wasn't wanting to go home.

He was wondering what he would say to Ann in the morning before he left. There wasn't much he could tell her of his real thoughts because he didn't quite know them himself. And he didn't have the right to try and tell her what they were. All he knew was that there would be a longing in him for her, a looking back on these days and a straining of memory to recall her every look and gesture, the sound of her voice.

He heard the courthouse door creaking open now, heard it shut gently. And abruptly he was feeling tired and let down, wanting nothing so much as to get back to the hotel and to sleep so as to forget and give his mind a rest. He was wishing Cromer would hurry.

He glanced across the walk looking for Cromer's lanky shape to emerge from the shadows under the portico. Abruptly a shadow did come down the steps. But, instead of it being Cromer, it was a shorter one, slender, familiar.

The instant he was sure it was Ann, he was leaving the saddle, dropping the reins.

She waited there on the walk for him. And as he came up to her the starlight let him catch a hint of the gladness and the wonder written on the pale oval of her face.

They stood that way a long moment, looking at each other

without speaking. Suddenly she breathed in a hushed voice, "Rush, come to me!" Then she was in his arms, her face tilting up to his, her lips meeting his.

This was what he had to live for. And as he drew her closer, feeling the giving in her, he knew that all the uncertainty and the emptiness of his tomorrows was gone.

Peter Dawson is the *nom de plume* used by Jonathan Hurff Glidden. He was born in Kewanee, Illinois, and was graduated from the University of Illinois with a degree in English literature. In his career as a Western writer, he published sixteen Western novels and over 120 Western novelettes and short stories for the magazine market. From the beginning, he was a dedicated craftsman who revised and polished his fiction until it shone as a fine gem. His Peter Dawson novels are noted for their adept plotting, interesting and well developed characters, their authentically researched historical backgrounds, and his stylistic flair. His first novel, *The Crimson Horseshoe,* won the Dodd, Mead Prize as the best Western of the year 1941 and ran serially in Street & Smith's *Western Story* prior to book publication. During the Second World War, Glidden served with the U.S. Strategic and Tactical Air Force in the United Kingdom. Later in 1950 he served for a time as Assistant to Chief of Station in Germany. After the war, his novels were frequently serialized in *The Saturday Evening Post.* Peter Dawson titles such as *High Country, Gunsmoke Graze,* and *Royal Gorge* are generally conceded to be among his masterpieces although he was an extremely consistent writer and virtually all his fiction has retained its classic stature among readers of all generations. One of Jon Glidden's finest techniques was his ability after the fashion of Dickens and Tolstoy to tell his stories via a series of dramatic vignettes which focus on a wide assortment of different characters, all tending to develop their own lives, situations, and predicaments, while at the same time propelling the general plot of the story toward a suspenseful conclusion. *Dark Riders of Doom* (1996), *Rattlesnake Mesa* (1997), and *Ghost Brand of the Wishbones* (1998) are his most recent titles.